LAKEBORN

Victoria Larque

BUTTERDRAGONS
PUBLISHING

Title: Lakeborn
Author: Victoria Larque
Copyright © 2022 Butterdragons® Publishing
All Rights Reserved

Published by Butterdragons® Publishing
https://butterdragons.com

ISBN: 9789493229570 (ebook)
ISBN: 9789493229587 (paperback)
ISBN: 9789493287181 (trade paperback)
ISBN: 9789493229594 (audio book)

Cover Design by: Dazed Designs

Audio book narrated by MJ Webb and Joshua Schubart

For those who dare to dream.

She is the Lake
And the Lake is her

The water runs through her veins
A power uniquely hers

The past is forgotten
A dark space full of questions
Memories lost forever

When the pain of not knowing
Becomes too heavy
She wades out into the lake
Submerging herself

Purifying her soul
Rejuvenating her body

Making her rejoice in peace
Becoming one with her Lake

by Helle Gade

Chapter One

Night never came easy. It was, as it had always been, greeted by a crescendo of cries, chirps, croaks, buzzing and twittering. It was the loudest time of day. The creatures of the lake and the forest surrounding it bade the day farewell and welcomed the darkness.

The last rays of light caressed the ripples on the water, dancing with it. They lit up the thousands of gnats that hovered around the banks, making them look like fireflies. They held little warmth, but they were beautiful. A dim light, a kind light. Light that did not blind or sting. It was soft, as soft as the touch of a floating dandelion seed. Almost not really there.

She knelt at the edge of the lake, prodding pebbles that looked different now, under the last rays of the sun. Golden and then red. A smile played on her lips when she found the perfect one. Round and flat, a bit sharp around the edges.

She got up and bent her knees, then, with a well-trained flick of her wrist and a subtle turn of her hips she let the stone loose. It skidded across the water.

"One, two, three, fourfivesixseven-ten-fourteen-twenty-one!" She jumped up and down, flinging her fists through the air and grinned. Her naked feet tapped the pebbled ground and made little splashing noises when they hit the water. Droplets clung to her legs and the torn edges of her dress.

Laughing, she twirled in a circle and let out yelps of joy. Then she formed a funnel to her mouth with both hands and shouted, cried, twittered and croaked through it. With that she elevated the crescendo of welcome, letting her voice mix with the countless others around her.

It was as it had always been and as it would always be.

Her dress fluttering and strands of her copper-red hair whirling, she ran along the bank of her lake. Her heart beat fast, thumping alongside the rhythm of her feet on the ground. Like music. She twined it with sweet humming and the clapping of her palms. Skipping up a small hill, she gazed at the last glimpse of the sun and then turned around.

This was a special night. She knew it from the way her bones sang and because of the full, round, yellow moon that was coming up. It was *her* special night. She sat down on the silky grass and waited.

The chill that crept up from the lake didn't make her shiver. It was a sweet chill, a moist, velvet coolness and she welcomed it. Like she did the night. Like she did the moon. The day was over, her night had come.

The yellow turned to silver as the moon ascended over her forest. It was time. She got up and peeled the straps from her dress off her shoulders. With a whisper of air, the dress slid down her body and pooled at her feet. One foot at a time she stepped from it.

Goosebumps flashed across her naked skin as she felt the silver light caress her. Closing her eyes, she walked down the hill. Slowly, quietly. Still the smile on her lips never wavered. This was a special night. The pull of her lake was strong now and she shivered with anticipation. But not yet.

The silver light reached the edge of the lake and made it shine. As they had before with the sun, the ripples now danced with this light. Silvery, cool, enchanting. She inched closer to the water, but held herself back. Not yet.

The sounds of the night creatures were softer, they subtly spoke of danger, of the hunt and of hiding. Her body swayed to their song of darkness and if she could have, she would have sung along. But she refrained from doing so. The shifting of her hips and curling of her arms were her only responses to the dark melody.

Silver light grew on the lake as the moon got higher. Soon it would cover all, soon she would pierce that glowing, sparkling veil. But not yet. The pull grew and she kept on swaying to the night song to keep herself distracted. But her bones began singing a different song now, a silvery, cool one and she lost her rhythm.

Mist crept over the rippling surface of her lake, shimmering in the light of the moon like a breath of frost. Like the breath from another world. She smiled at it in greeting and filled her lungs to bursting as the light finally covered all. The whole lake was illuminated and she felt the pull increase to an almost painful degree.

Her body shook and she had trouble placing one foot in front of the other. Her body wanted to run, to fling itself into the water. But she forced it to be slow, forced it to last longer. When her toes touched the surface, the ripples thrown back started to glow. It wasn't the light of the moon, it was a multitude of colors. Illuminated blue, shiny green and glowing silver. Her ankles were greeted by the chilly water, then her legs and finally her thighs. She waded deeper, her face and pale body aglow with the colors her presence revealed.

A long breath trembled from her lips as the water reached her belly. It was cold, but she kept going. The deeper she got, the more the pressure inside her grew. The water teased her breasts and the skin beneath her collarbone, like the caress of a lover. The soft ripples nipped and kissed at her neck, her chin, her lips, her cheeks, her eyelids and the top of her head. Submerged as she was now, little bubbles rose from her mouth. The strange glow seeped into her, it flooded out of her. It surrounded her and grew out. Until the whole lake shimmered with luminous blue, shiny green and glowing silver.

The creatures of the night held their breaths, gazing at the lake. Forgotten was the hunt, the search for food and the hiding. With small and big, beating hearts, they waited. They waited and watched as the woman floated through the depths, illuminating them, as she was illuminated herself.

Then, like a deep sigh, like the heaving of an enormous chest, a tremor ran through the lake. It stretched out through the forest, making the trees rustle and sway and then was sucked back to the lake. From one second to the next, the tension vanished. The glow dimmed until it was gone and the creatures of the night turned from the sight and continued their song.

She let out a sigh of her own. Her body felt light as she floated on her back and looked at the moon. Giggling she turned, dove under and shot upwards. She hummed and splashed, fanned out her hair, rubbed at the dirt on her fingers and floated a bit more. The pressure on her body had turned to a relaxing thrum of power – the power of the lake – beating against her skin. Not forcefully, but light and pulsing. It was hers as well. The power of the deep, the energy of all life surrounding it.

It made her strong, it healed cuts and bruises in seconds and it listened to her command. Without her the lake held no power beyond its waters and she held none without it. She was as much part of its cold depths as it was part of her smiling lips and fluttering hair.

****

She floated still and reveled in the pulsing power and the light of the moon as a sound had her jerking upright. A sound so foreign that she swam toward it.

It was the sound of snapping and breaking wood, the sound of feet slapping the ground and of cloth rubbing and scratching along branches and leaves. She felt the rhythm of a foreign heart, the running of a stranger's feet, and the ragged, harsh breath of a deep chest.

A human. Anger swelled inside her overwhelming her mind and heart. It burned in her veins and made her fists shake. She had met those before. They did nothing but destroy, sully and desecrate what they got their hands on. Every few years they tried to settle around her lake. At first, she had been curious, but after seeing what they were capable of, after knowing the dark depths of their greedy hearts, she had cast them out. And all those that came after the first ones.

Most of them had returned, with fire and steel. She had doused their fire and used their steel to cut them. And so, they had run, those that had been left alive. They thought of her as a demon, a ghost, something dangerous and not from this world. They were wrong on all accounts.

The last settlers had been long ago, and she sometimes wondered if this lake being protected was finally known across its borders. So why was this human running toward her lake? At night no less?

Her head snapped up as she heard more footsteps, more beating hearts and more ragged breaths. They were chasing the other human. She frowned, not understanding. They chased animals and they had chased her, but each other? Where lay the sense in that?

The human reached the bank of her lake and she trembled as his foot hit the water. It invaded her, as much as a touch would. Coppery droplets of his blood splashed the surface, mixing with the water. Soiling it. She ground her teeth and swam in his direction. He needed to get out of her lake, away from her forest. Now.

The water lapped at his knees when he halted to look back. The other men broke through the trees and came to a halt before the lake. Their eyes roamed over the water and settled on him.

He hunched over in defeat, his breath wheezing and his body leaking more blood into the water.

Raising one hand at the others, he spoke. "Fine," another wheezing breath, "you've caught me. Now what?"

A big human stepped forward and grinned evilly. "Now you'll feed the fishes, boy." He got out a long piece of steel that was oddly shaped and waved it at the man in the water. A bang loud as thunder sounded. It echoed through the forest and made her ears hurt. The man in the water clutched his chest and fell back. The water around him grew dark fast.

The woman pulled at the power of the water, readying herself to attack the men. No one sullied her lake. She felt the smooth ground beneath her feet. Felt the mud squeeze out between her toes as she got up. The water sloshed from her body, leaving only her thighs and legs covered in it.

The men saw her and took a step back.

"What the fuck?" the big one uttered. The shiny piece of steel swiveled and pointed at her.

"Leave here," she said. The angry sound of her words felt foreign and uncomfortable on her tongue. "Leave and do not come back."

A laugh shook the air as the big man doubled over. "What is this? Some fucking nudist hideaway?"

She grabbed hold of the power and threw it outward. "Leave, I said!" The power flung the men back like a punch, they sailed through the air, hitting trees and rolling over in the pebbles covering her bank. She walked forward and loosened gushes of pressure their way, hitting them in the chest, the back, everywhere. The big man groaned and turned, he leveled the piece of steel to her chest and another bang sounded through the night.

A force hit her shoulder and she could hear bones splinter. It did not dim her rage. She blasted the men into the forest as far as she could.

She huffed and snarled, then listened. It seemed like they were running as if a demon was at their tails. Nodding once, she went back to the water. Placing her hand over the hole in her shoulder she attempted to heal herself, but the wound would not close. Putting one finger into the wound, she stifled a groan as she felt there was something lodged inside it. Dipping her shoulder under water, she used the pull of the lake to get out whatever was inside her.

A soft cry escaped her lips as a tiny, round pebble of steel fell into her hand. She tossed it and heard the clinking sound it made as it hit the small stones on the bank.

This time, her bones and skin knit together smoothly. But the coppery taste on her tongue did not vanish and she felt an uncomfortable pressure somewhere. She turned and saw the man still floating on her lake. She breathed in deeply and waded to him. With a crinkled nose, she started to pull him to shore. He was done soiling her lake.

A grunt from behind her had her turning her head. He seemed to be still alive. She squinted at the wound on his chest. A glow came from it, an illuminating blue, a shiny green and a glowing silver. No that could not be, could it?

The lake was healing him. But why? It had never healed a human before. She should toss him to the edge of her forest and be done with it. She really should. But she stood rooted to the spot and watched as his wound closed. He started squirming and his lids fluttered. He was waking. She hissed and punched him. He went still again.

She was not yet ready to decide what to do with him. No matter what the lake had done. He had ruined her special night. He had invaded and soiled her lake. And it had healed him. She frowned and picked up his feet to drag him further. She lay him down on the grass and then sat down next to him.

Watching the moon and her glittering lake, listening to the night song that had picked up again, she pondered on what to do with this intruder.

Chapter Two

She hugged her knees to her chest and dug up soft dirt with her toes between the grass. Her lips gently rested on one knee and from time to time, she would purse them and then nibble softly at her skin. She tasted of water, and a bit of copper.

Scowling, she lay her cheek down on her knee and eyed the human next to her. His breath came in regular bursts now and he was close to waking. Still, she had not decided. She knew only one thing – she would not kill him. The lake had healed him and even if she did not understand why, it would be a waste of energy if she took his life now. Maybe he would just wake up and leave, that would be for the best.

Extending one leg, she prodded him with her foot. He felt strange. Warm. Rolling her eyes at her own curiosity, she gave up and crouched over him. She had not seen a human this close before, had not touched one. Not for a very long time. So long in fact, that she could not remember clearly.

His dark shirt was dirty, bloody, and wet. Where were the buttons? Were there not supposed to be buttons? She found none. The fabric clung to his body like a second skin and she nudged his chest with a finger. She looked down her own. She had thought men had no breasts whatsoever, that there was only bones and skin. But his rose subtly from his chest. She prodded him again. It felt like nothing more than an extra layer of muscle. The soft but firm muscles covered most of him. His stomach was littered with them. She poked at her own. It was flat and smooth. Picking up his shirt she took a glance underneath. Snorting, she let it fall again immediately. He had hair on his stomach, not much, only a line from his belly button downwards. It still reminded her of a furry animal.

And what was that? His arms were as broad as her thighs, his hands twice as big as hers, at least. She hadn't known humans were this big. She lay down next to him and frowned. If he were to stand, she would come up to his chest, with the top of her head.

She sat up again and took him in with a long, hard look. He was huge compared to her. And she had seen even bigger ones. Pursing her lips, she reached for the mop of brown, disheveled hair that covered his face. Revealing it, she tilted her head to the side. His features were even. His nose was straight and his lips curved delicately, the lower one was fuller. His eyebrows were a shade darker than his hair and he had stubble across his chin and around his mouth. She reached out and stroked a finger over it. It was rough and scratchy. A smile nudged at her lips. There was nothing rough or scratchy on her own body. And she knew from the mirror image of her face on the lake that he had more hard edges to his face than she did.

Curious. She had known that she differed from them. But she hadn't known how much. Wriggling her toes, she wondered if he had ten as well, if he had any at all. What did he look like under those clothes?

Scowling she drew up her knees again. It did no good musing about it. As soon as he woke, he would leave. She had plenty to occupy herself with, she didn't need to be distracted.

Thinking of which – she spied a mouse in the grass. Smiling, she watched as its nose twitched and twisted, making the whiskers vibrate, while the hairy little ears were pressed back against its fur. One scuttle at a time, it worked its way around. Sniffing out food and listening for enemies. Its little heart fluttered with awareness as the tiny paws made next to no sound on the silvery grass.

A bug buzzed by, twirling in awkward circles before falling down onto the ground with a soft plop. She giggled. Bugs always seemed to have no idea where they were going and they had a rather peculiar way of getting there.

Breathing in the scent of earth, wet grass, flowers and the water she flopped down on her back. She twirled a strand of her hair with one finger as she watched the moon. It was in the middle of the sky now and much smaller than it had been. The light still felt like a caress, a cold one but she liked it. She liked the way it made everything look different. Magical. Her skin, the lake, the forest. She loved how her wet skin would glow and twinkle when she swam. She sighed and eyed the water longingly. Then she scowled at the man. When would he wake?

****

His head hurt like shit and his eyes felt as if a car had parked on his lids. His chest hurt and he lifted one hand to search for the bullet hole. That's right, Gus had shot him. *Piece of work.* That man was such a sore loser. He groaned as his muscles rebelled. His hand felt for the wound but found nothing. *What the heck?*

He remembered it clear as day. The bang, the impact, the cold water against his back. Floating. Why was he lying on grass? With a grunt, he forced open his eyes. The first thing he saw was the full moon. He sat in the middle of the sky in all his big, fat roundness.

Blinking and groaning he pushed himself up to look at his chest. There had to be a wound somewhere.

19

Lifting the collar of his shirt, he peeked down his chest. Nothing. His index finger fiddled with the hole in his shirt. There it was, the bullet hole. But underneath was nothing but smooth skin, no scar, no scabs. Nothing.

He must have hit his head or something. He looked up and jerked back. A red-headed woman sat a few feet away. He blinked, she was naked.

Not that he could see anything, she had her knees pulled up to her chest and only her side faced him. Her dark eyes watched him warily. Her hair fell down her entire back in untidy strands and pooled on the grass.

Apart from looking a bit disheveled, she was the most beautiful creature he had ever seen. Her eyes shimmered like the lake behind her, they were bottomless as they drew him in. He felt he could stare at them forever. Drown in them. Her face was like that of a porcelain doll, with a feral edge and something utterly feminine. The slender and pale fingers that she'd folded over her knees were delicate and looked fragile. She seemed young, maybe in her mid-twenties.

"Am I dead?" he asked.

She snorted. It was strange hearing her make such a harsh sound. "I wish," she uttered. Her voice was melodic and surprisingly deep. It was like a caress. He shook his head. What was he thinking? A voice like a caress? Eyes he could drown in? He must've hit his head damned hard.

Wait a minute, had she just said 'I wish'?

"Excuse me?"

She frowned. "If you were dead, I would have my peace. You have ruined my night by bleeding into my lake and bringing along all those other humans. Humans *I* had to take care of."

Was this woman for real? Humans? Humans she had taken care of? And what did she mean he'd ruined her night?

"Back up honey, who did you take care of? Who are you and how the bloody hell am I not dead?"

He licked his dry lips and rubbed his temples. This headache was killing him.

She glowered at him. "The men you led here. I had to toss them out of my forest. I do not care much for having the likes of you around." She huffed and looked down. "And you are not dead because the lake healed you. Why it did so, I have no idea." At the last sentence, her voice rose and echoed over the lake, as if she wasn't talking to him. As if she wanted the lake to hear her anger.

This was getting stranger by the minute. God, his head hurt. He wished it would stop so that he could think clearly for a second.

She unfolded her slim legs and got up, flashing him with a tantalizing view. "Now, if you would kindly go away. I have things that need attending."

He stared. She did nothing to shield her body from his view and it was quite a view. Not that it did anything for him at the moment. His head occupied his mind nearly completely. But if it had been in a better condition... Scratch that. He forced his pounding head down. He might be an opportunist and a hustler, but he wasn't a complete ass. He swallowed. This was a dream, it had to be. No way he had been shot just to wake to the sight and accusations of an otherworldly beautiful woman. Somehow, he had thought heaven would be more welcoming.

Not that he believed in heaven, much less that he would end up there after his death. But come on. She did kind of look like a little angel. Unkempt and angry, but radiantly beautiful.

"Could you... Ah... Could you put some clothes on, sweetheart? This is rather uncomfortable for me."

"Fine," she said. "But then you leave."

What sort of an answer was that? He could see her feet walk a few paces and then she picked up something off the ground. He heard the rustling of fabric and then she walked back to him.

"There, dressed. Now leave."

He looked up again. The dress she wore was white, or it had been once. It was shredded at the hem and dirty. Still, the way she held herself was almost regal. The defiant jutting of her chin, the delicate line of her neck, the way she pushed back her shoulders. She was still the most amazing woman he had ever seen.

He tried to get up, but the moment he moved his head, it felt like a drill was tackling it. Groaning, he slumped back down.

"Don't think I can."

"What is that supposed to mean? Just get up and start walking. Back to wherever it is you came from."

He looked up at her. A scowl graced her face – she was dead serious.

"Listen, sweetheart. I'll just crash here for the night, okay? It doesn't look like rain and if Gus and his men are really gone, you'll be safe. I'll go once I can stand. Promise."

She tilted her head to the side once, seemingly pondering his words. Then she nodded. "Tomorrow you leave."

"Sure thing, sweetheart," he mumbled and let his torso sink into the grass again. He closed his eyes against the pain and hoped that he would either die or wake up from this messed up dream. But then, he wouldn't see her again if he died, or woke. He pushed one arm under his head, tilting it up a bit and opened his eyes.

She sat on the grass and watched her twitching toes. Then she got up and skipped to the water. As if she had forgotten about him, she splashed around. She twirled in circles and chased after a few fireflies.

He had no idea how long he watched her dance, twirl and skip, it could have been hours or minutes, but her antics had an enchanting quality and even through the headache, he was unable to look away. The woman skipped up the hill again. She threw him an angry glance. then curled up on the grass a few feet away.

The headache drummed along to his heartbeat and he felt his lids get heavy. Pity, he would have liked to see her again. This strange, angry, insane beauty. But he knew she was too much to be real. Too perfect. Too strange. His mangled brain was making him hallucinate. That was the only explanation. Listening to her soft and even breaths he soon fell asleep.

Chapter Three

The song of her lake changed subtly as dawn made the stars disappear. One by one, they vanished from view as the sky lit up slowly. She waved at the twinkling specs of light and smiled. Then she stretched out her arms and yawned extensively.

The sun had not yet breached the horizon, but the birds already chirped a welcome. She began humming her own song of welcome as she sat up and rubbed the sleep from her eyes. A look to her right silenced her. He was still there. Lying on her hill. Sleeping. She frowned as she waited for anger to overtake her mind. But it didn't come. The only thing she could muster was slight annoyance and... curiosity.

A loud snore had her jerking back. By the water, he made strange sounds in his sleep. Was he dying? She listened. No, his heart beat steady and strong, his breaths came even, if a bit too loud. She shook her head and got up.

The human seemed to have an aversion to naked skin, so she decided to take her swim now, before he woke. She could not wait until he left. She needed to feel the water around her now. Skipping to the shore, she undid her dress and waded into the deep.

A sigh left her lips as shivers raked her skin. It was cold so early in the morning and the pain the chill left in her lungs was delicious. She shot through the water like a fish. Weightless. Content. At home. Little nips tickled her feet and legs. She giggled as she looked down and saw the swarm of baby fish around her. They had been born a few weeks ago, she had watched them hatch and now they sometimes accompanied her swims. She carefully stroked one and smiled at the smooth feel of his scaly dress. So soft, so silky.

From one second to the next, they were gone. She turned to look down, knowing what had scared them away. She wriggled her fingers at the large fish underneath her. His sharp teeth showed as he opened and closed his mouth. His dark body was freckled with bright spots all over. He was half her size and an old friend. She knew him since his birth. Which was about twenty years ago.

"Hello, having a good morning?" she asked him.

He opened and closed his mouth a few times and then sped through the water like an arrow, no doubt in pursuit of the baby-fish that had surrounded her a minute ago.

"Don't eat too many now, you're getting fat," she called after him. She seldom interfered with the cycle of life and death around her. It always ended up getting too close. And nature worked that way. Everything around her was fleeting. Only she and the lake were permanent. She did keep the balance. For everything she took, she gave something in return.

She nursed wounded animals back to health and then she let them go. Having a friend around from time to time was enough, but eventually they all left or grew old and died. She had long since distanced herself from the notion of a constant companion. It just never happened and if you cared for another being enough to love it, then its demise was all the more painful. She loved them all, but she had learned to love them with a distance. It was safer for her heart that way.

Flipping back her legs, she turned and dove to the ground. She crouched down and kicked off as hard as she could. Shooting to the surface she yelled out in joy as her face pierced the glimmering veil. How she loved this. The water, her lake, her one permanent companion. As deep and powerful as her own soul.

But today, something was off. She enjoyed her swim, but something drove her back to shore, something nudging at the back of her mind. The human and her curiosity for him. He had spoken to her last night, in a strange accent and with foreign words. Why had he stared at her so raptly? And why had the view of his open eyes startled her so? They had captured hers in a way that was akin to the view of her lake at sunset. But that could not be. Maybe it had been her special night and the fact that her lake had healed him. There could be no other explanation.

She swiped back her hair with both hands and smiled at the feel of the water running down her body. It tickled. Glancing at the hill she could see that he was still asleep. She pulled the dress over her wet skin, so she would not offend him again when he woke. She wondered briefly why she even cared if he was offended but shrugged it off.

It was time to find some food. She hastened across the pebbled ground, feeling each stone digging into her soles with absolute clarity. It was not uncomfortable. She jumped into the grass and felt it tickle her thighs and lower legs as she walked to the line of trees at the edge of her forest. Here, the floor was soft and she dug her toes in between the moss and the thicket of leaves. Kicking up her foot, she made them flutter up and she made a game of trying to catch some of the leaves while they came down.

A doe stood a few feet away and eyed her antics. She smiled at her, this one was carrying her second babe and it seemed as though the little one was to come soon.

"Do not worry, love, I will have an eye on you when it is time." She winked and the doe continued to nibble on a batch of leaves, licking the dew from their slick green surfaces. Her bottomless, big eyes didn't leave her though.

She grinned and hopped off. Twirling between the trees and humming along to the twittering of birds she came across what she was looking for. A little cluster of mushrooms. She picked up a branch that had fallen from a tree and snapped it in half. She tossed one and let her thumb graze the sharp edge of the other. This would do fine. She cut the heads off, leaving the stems in the ground. Normally she would take three and leave the rest. But she had a guest now, so she took six.

****

He woke to the soft splashing of waves and the tickling of sunlight on his face. Opening his eyes, he noticed that his headache was gone. Completely. As were all the aches of his body, even the one in his lower back that had developed after his month of working on a construction site. He had left after the job was done, the ache hadn't. Eventually, he'd gotten used to it. Now, it was gone.

He sat up and groaned. He was still sitting on the hill he remembered from last night. The sun was peeking over the line of trees and he wondered if last night had really happened. He had gotten shot, only to wake with a pounding headache and a naked woman next to him. A woman that had been as beautiful as she had been insane. He shook his head, clearing it from the last bits of sleep. Then he searched his chest again. Just like last night he came up with nothing, except for the hole in his shirt.

So, it hadn't been a dream and he hadn't died. That was a plus, but now what? He had no idea where he was. His car had broken down in the middle of nowhere and he had fled on foot from Gus and his men. He could be anywhere.

He pulled his phone from his pocket but it was a bust. It had not survived the dip in the lake. Figured. Wait a minute, if it hadn't been a dream, then the woman had to be here somewhere. She should know where 'here' was. His eyes scanned the lake and its banks but he didn't see anything. He got up and walked down the hill to the water. Crouching down, he splashed his face.

A sweet melody had him turning his head and there she was. She skipped from between the trees, her long hair trailing behind her like copper ribbons. She was every bit as ethereal and unbelievable as he remembered. And he wondered how she had 'taken care' of Gus and his men. Maybe they had just left after they thought he was dead.

He shook his head. True, he had messed with Gus, but he hadn't thought the guy would go overboard and leave him for the fishes. Nothing explained why he had no wound though.

He watched as she came closer and with every skip she took, he became more enthralled by her appearance. Her eyes sparkled with light, just like the lake did in the sun, and her slender legs carried her gracefully and without fail across the shore. As if she had run this way a thousand times. Hell, maybe she had, how would he know?

"I see you have woken," she said as she reached him. Again, he marveled at the sound of her voice before he grasped what she'd said.

"Yeah." He got up and looked at her. "What have you got there?" he asked pointing to her hands.

She spread them out. "Food."

"Mushrooms? Are you sure they're not poisonous?"

She snorted as if that question was ridiculous, and maybe to her it was.

"You want some?"

He was taken aback. Last night she had been adamant that he left and now she wanted him to have breakfast with her? Strange creature. But he nodded, his stomach was rumbling and he wasn't able to look away from her. Being here with her a bit longer couldn't hurt. So, he nodded and followed her up to the hill they had slept on.

The subtle sway of her hips was captivating and he appreciated the way it increased as she began to ascend. He shook his head, he was leaving after they had eaten. But he found that maybe he didn't want to, not right away, at least.

She sat down on the grass and handed him three mushroom caps along with some sort of root when he did the same. He glanced at the things and then looked at her. She was already nibbling on the root while watching him. Did she live out here all by herself? Where was her house?

"What's your name?" he asked.

She tilted her head to the side, exposing the pale skin of her neck. "Name?"

"Yes, you have a name, don't you? I'm Christian, but my friends call me Chris."

"Christian." Hearing her say his name made something inside him jerk, but he couldn't for the life of him tell what it was. He only knew that it affected him.

"And yours?"

She shook her head. "No one calls me by a name."

He frowned. "That can't be right. Even if you were some feral, wild child, you can talk, so you must have learned it from someone. What do your parents call you?"

"I have none. If I ever had any, I cannot remember them."

Again, the more she said the more confused he got. "But you can speak and you... How did you get here? Where are you from? Who are you?"

She scrutinized him silently and he had the same feeling from last night swallow him. The feeling that he was sinking into her eyes, drowning. They had a strange color, a mix of green and blue, and it felt as if he was exposed underneath her gaze.

"I have always been here. This is my home and it has always been thus."

Okay, his theory that she was insane was backed. She didn't seem disoriented though, or in any other way mad. Apart from the skipping and singing and not having a name. Maybe she just needed help, to get back into civilization or something.

"Eat, I will not have you waste anything." She nodded at the mushrooms.

He started to nibble on one, it tasted surprisingly good. "You want to come with me when I leave? I could show you the city."

She smiled. "No. As I have told you, I do not care much for the likes of your kind."

"My kind? Do you mean men?"

"No, I mean humans."

He stared. "But you're human."

She laughed. It was a silvery and bright sound. "I am most definitely not."

"What else are you then?" he asked as he decided to play along, curious as to how far she was prepared to take this.

"I am the Lady of the Lake of course, silly man. Just as I have always been."

"Of course, you are." He scowled at her. "Now, kindly cut the crap, sweetheart. This madness has gone on far too long. Who are you really?"

She frowned at him. "I did not understand all you just said, but I would ask that you leave now. I will not sit by idly while you insult me, no matter if the lake has healed you." A strange pressure radiated from her and he felt as if it pushed at him. What the hell? The color of her eyes seemed to move, to swirl, and he scrambled back. That look felt like the lash of a whip and fear crept into his heart. How could such a small and beautiful creature radiate such a feeling of danger?

"Leave, now," her voice echoed and made him jump.

He held up his hands and stood up. "Easy, I'm sorry, okay? I'll leave." He walked down the hill and jogged to the forest. His mind scrambled but good.

Chapter Four

His heart hammered when he stepped through the trees. *What the hell had just happened?* Chris frowned. That could not have been real, the way her eyes had darkened and her whole being had seemed to suck away the light around her, leaving only that feeling of imminent danger. That pressure that had come off her, pushing at him.

He shook his head, he had clearly imagined that. What else could it have been? Still, the fear hitting him in that moment was hard to shake.

As he trudged on, the ground soft beneath his feet, he noticed something strange. His chest pulsed slightly, right where he should have had a gunshot wound. The pulsing grew into pressure and then into something close to pain. His hand rubbed over the spot. There was nothing, only smooth skin. But the more he walked, the more painful it got.

He sighed and stopped. His life had taken a turn into a pretty shitty direction yesterday. Leading up to now. To this strange place and this even stranger woman. Why did his chest hurt? He hadn't felt a thing since he'd woken up last night, to a pounding headache and a naked, ethereal woman. A woman without a name, who was clearly deranged. *The Lady of the Lake*? She had to be completely out of it.

But to be honest, he was very much to blame for ending up here. He'd screwed up, royally. Because he had forgotten the most basic rule: Never outstay your welcome.

He sank back against the trunk of a tree and sat down. There was no way to tell where he was and he had no idea how to get back to where he came from. Not that he wanted to go there, but still. Hell, he didn't even know which way he had come last night. It had been dark and he'd been chased. Yeah, that was his fault as well.

Chris tried to breathe past the pain in his chest and let his head sink back against the tree. He closed his eyes and was sucked back into memories.

He had woken in a cheap motel room yesterday in the arms of a woman he didn't know, where the duvet smelled strange and the curtains hung heavy with dirt and years-worth of cigarette smoke. The linoleum floor was cracked in some places and bloated out in others. But he hadn't cared.

It'll be over soon. Those words had kept him sane since... Well, since forever actually. But it was never over. None of it was. When he'd changed families more frequently than underwear as a kid, he'd told himself it would be over eventually. And it was, apart from the scars on his body and on his soul. Mementos from a time that had been shittier than he cared to remember. He had gotten out of it, his mind hadn't, not for a while at least.

Falling in with a gang and walking the path of easy money had seemed like a good choice back then. But Chris had not cared much for the inner workings of the gang and soon he'd decided to go freelancing. He took all the tricks he'd learned from his time with crooks and thieves and tweaked them a bit.

He'd traveled around, never staying too long in one place and for a time, he'd made decent money off his cons. Enough to get to the next place, at least. He knew that his face was pretty enough to fool almost anyone and his hands were quick, his mind sharp. But yesterday, he'd bitten off more than he could chew.

He had woken, showered, dressed and headed out, leaving the woman to her own devices. The local gambling hall was easy prey. Small town, old technology. Easy as pie. Then his eyes and his focus had wandered to the poker tables. And that right there had been it. The start of his royal screw-up.

The table had been almost full when he'd joined, but it had not stayed that way. His hardest opponent, Gus, had. Chris had noticed the harshness in the man's eyes, the calculating coldness. but like a fool, he hadn't worried. His car had been filled up already and the moment he left the casino, he'd planned on skipping town.

Screwing over the criminal lord of the town had been a very bad idea, screwing his sister had been even worse. But Chris had not known who she was, he had not known who Gus was. Now, he knew. Gus's sister had done a double take when she had joined her brother at the table to bring him a drink. And Chris had known it was bad the moment the woman he had woken up next to whispered something to the opponent he was currently fleecing. The moment the big man's lips had turned into a fine line and his eyes had grown murderous.

He had somehow escaped to his car, but not for long. Fleeing that bunch of crazy-ass idiots he had wound up here. In the middle of bloody nowhere.

He rubbed at his chest again, the pain was not lessening. He grunted and got up, but wasn't able to take a single step further. The pain in his chest was searing and made it impossible to move.

Frowning, he tried to take a step back. That worked. What the hell? Chris turned and tentatively took another step. The pain didn't seem as bad as before. He turned the other way again and two strides further he couldn't move, again.

So, he wasn't imagining this. An icy tingle shot up his spine and made him tremble. Something wasn't right, not by a long shot. Rooted to the spot, he debated what he was going to do next. His mind was having trouble coming up with a reason, an explanation.

"Why are you still here? I told you to leave, did I not?" her voice was melodic, soft and entrancing, it was the sweetest and purest voice he had ever heard. Even wrought with anger, it was all of the above.

He sighed. "I would if I could, sweetheart. And I know this is gonna sound strange, but I can't move past that tree right there."

He pointed at the heavy oak tree he had tried to pass. The woman floated, for lack of a better word, past him and looked at the tree. Her delicate brows were drawn as she stroked her hands across the bark. He could see her shoulders sag in some sort of defeat. Like the weight of the world was pulling at her.

"It would seem you are right," she whispered.

"Excuse me," Chris asked. He was flabbergasted. She just... believed him?

The woman turned and looked at him, an angry gleam in her eyes. "The lake healed you. It feeds the forest around us, up to this three. Beyond that it holds no power and it takes what has been given."

Chris stared at her, she was out of her goddamned mind. He didn't understand half of what she had meant, but she was implying – no, that could not be.

"Whatever sweetheart. I'll just try again." He walked to the tree, determined to get away from her, from this forest and this strange, cold tingle that was running along his spine.

"Christian," she breathed. He ignored her.

"If you leave, you will die."

That got his attention. "You know, this isn't funny anymore," he said, real fear flaring to life inside him. He was not easy to scare, his experiences had hardened him. But this made his heart ice up and sharp fear clog his airways. "This has been fun until now, sweetheart, but you can stop with the games now."

He was grappling for control, his mind running around in circles. And he knew that a panic attack wasn't far away. He hadn't had one since he'd been sixteen years old.

The woman shook her head, a scowl on her beautiful face. "By all means, try it. I have no use for you. I just thought you could use the warning." She glided past him, her slender feet not making a sound on the ground. When she stood next to him, she looked into his face.

"I will go now. If you want to try and leave, you will die in the process. I do not care for your presence, but I will not drive you out by force. Feel free to either stay or die." She walked away. "It is your choice."

Chris cursed as he watched her walk from him, he looked back at the tree, back at her and cursed again.

"Hold up. I'm coming with you."

The woman stilled and her straight back seemed to freeze in place. "It seems to be the safer bet for you."

Yeah, he wasn't so sure about that, but he followed her, nonetheless. What else was he supposed to do?

****

"I can't just call you 'Lady'," the confounding and frustrating human said.

He had not asked about the lake, he had not asked about why he would die if he left. It had to be hard for him to think on it. Humans didn't believe. Even if they saw, even if they felt, they still chose not to believe. They rationalized things away that could not be explained. She pitied and despised them for that. Blind, stumbling children. With too much brains for their own good and too little to be of any good to everything else.

"I do not care what you call me," she said, stepping on a patch of soft moss. A smile grew on her face at the feel of it, but it did not last.

"I think I'll give you a name then."

Typical. He was not able to rationalize or explain what had happened to him, so he opted for deflection. She was strangely curious to see how far that would take him.

"Suit yourself."

"Amanda? No, that doesn't fit." His feet made loud noises as he blundered along at her side. Twigs cracked, making her flinch every time. "Ashley? No, maybe Jekaterina, or Natasha."

His babbling and stomping made a headache come along swiftly.

"Jane, you know, the girlfriend from that guy in the loincloth who swings around on vines?"

She ignored him.

"You don't know either of them, do you? It would kind of fit you though."

She closed her eyes and took a deep breath, trying to keep the annoyance and the headache at bay that he inspired with his antics. Maybe she should just leave him behind and try to live around him. The forest was big enough to hide and avoid him, but then she would not be able to keep an eye on him if he resorted to his human nature.

"Where are we going?"

A smile took form on her face, he *had* noticed them heading in a different direction than the lake. It seemed he wasn't completely useless.

"There is a storm coming," she answered. "We will need to get to shelter before sundown."

Chris squinted at the clear, blue sky, shading his eyes with a palm. "What are you talking about? There isn't a cloud up there."

"The wind has picked up and has gotten cooler. You will see clouds soon enough." She did not tell him how she understood the hum of the forest How she felt the energy of every living being around them. That every step on the ground, every heartbeat she felt, was filled with secrets. And she understood what each meant.

The trees thinned out somewhat as they began ascending a hill. The ground was harder now and littered with pieces of rock, which pierced the ground like deformed, gray mushrooms. The higher they got, the less trees and the more rocks and stones appeared.

Rounding a boulder, they came to the entrance of a cave. She had often resorted to this place if the weather had gotten bad. A few winters, she had shared it with a bear, those had been the warmest ones she could remember. A deep, rumbling companion, a friend. But the bear had died when her time had come, as everything always did. Still, the memories of this place were fond ones. It took her a distance away from her lake, but she could see its surface glimmer in the sunlight and the sight always warmed her.

"So, this is where you live?" the human asked.

"Sometimes," she answered and sat down on the stony ground.

He stepped around the cave, his fists on his hips, examining it. "Well, it doesn't go back too deep, but it could be cozier."

Sighing, she got up again, not knowing why she even bothered. "Stay here. I will find you something to

make it 'cozier'," with that she sprang away, leaving him
to his own devices.

Chapter Five

Her feet carried her down the hill in a flash, not stopping her from stroking across the bark of every tree she passed. Healthy trees, their leaves dancing with the wind that grew colder now. She felt goosebumps rise on her arms and smiled. The chilly wind carried the scent of rain, the promise of a storm. It was about time, her lake had shrunken from the pebbled banks considerably, these past few weeks.

She hung right, letting the lake pass on her left. Her steps faltered, her feet reluctant to carry on, but she would not have it. After a few minutes, she reached her destination and stopped. Her toes dug into the ground and her fingers pulled on the torn edges of her dress. She did not like this place. Painful memories brimmed the edges of her mind when she was here. Memories that she had hidden so deeply, there was no telling what they were. All she knew was that they spoke of agony.

Still, she forced her feet forward, past the broken, mossy ruins of huts and houses. The wooden beams cracked and poking skyward, like the bones of great beasts.

She should have taken the chest from here a long time ago. She should have... but something had stopped her, so she could force herself back here at least once a year. Maybe it was because she needed to see, needed to know they were gone, driven out by someone, or something.

She took in a trembling breath and stroked her palms across her upper arms as if to warm herself. Pressing her lids shut for a second, she gathered her will and then snapped them open again. A little heart beat at her feet and she looked down, a rabbit sat next to her, gazing up with huge, inquisitive eyes. One ear stood straight while the other hung down halfway.

"Are you coming with me, little one?" she asked.

As if to answer, his nose twitched and he hobbled off, in the direction of the last house still standing. She followed him. Each step took her back to a time long past. To flashes of memories she knew not what to make of. One night, it had been a night of... flames and terror.

Humans. They were unparalleled in their cruelty, to both their own, and to that which they did not understand. So why, by the dark depths of her lake, was she venturing here, to make a *human* more comfortable? The answer was not clear, she did not even know if there was one, but she was here now and not about to waste this opportunity.

With memories weighing down on her, whispers of past words, and a night darker than any before or after, she climbed the broken steps to the house.

Witch.

Kill her! Kill the witch!

Filthy, ungodly, whore! Spawn of Satan!

She bit her lower lip until she tasted leaden rust – blood. The memories were fluent, fuzzy and hard to hold onto, but the words... they were as clear and loud in her ears as they had been on that night. As was the fear icing along her veins, growing over her heart, making it hurt and her breath short. A fear that slowed everything down around her, pulling things into focus and blurring out others.

The sound of angry footsteps, the sound of flames licking at the air, the screams of a woman that was her and not her at the same time. A name...

She shook her head, flinging the memories out.

Deep, green eyes looking at her, a hand filled with mushrooms. "What's your name?"

"A name..." she muttered, fighting the fear and entering the house. "My name?" She looked around and found the rabbit waiting for her in front of the chest, the chest she had come here for. She tilted her head at the bundle of fluff. "Did I have a name?"

He stroked one paw over his crooked ear and glanced at her.

"I had a name... I remember. I had one... once."

A stinging pain in her temples made her gasp and clasp her head in her hands. The wave of agony had her sinking to her knees. Something beyond the pain was nudging at her, a wave of unfathomable magnitude. A wave of memories more painful than anything she could imagine.

"No!" She flung open the metal chest and pulled out a few blankets and fur, then she slammed it shut and stood on shaky legs. "Come on, little one," she told the rabbit while she stumbled from the room and out of the house.

As if being chased by demons, she sprinted through the rows of houses, tears of distress running down her cheeks, falling into oblivion. The wave of memories was following her, as was the headache. She didn't stop until she was far into the forest, where she collapsed on a patch of moss.

Her breath was ragged, sweat beaded on her forehead and she pressed her face into the blankets sobbing. This time, they were tears of relief – the memories hadn't followed, only the pain and fear had. There was no telling how long she lay there, shivering, trying to get a hold of herself.

The rumble of thunder and whipping tendrils of wind made her lift her head. She came face to nose with the little rabbit, who nudged her with his quivering whiskers. The little guy scuttled back when she sat up and looked at her quizzically. She smiled at him, blinking back the remainder of tears clinging to her lashes.

"That was something, it was it not?" She swiped her face with a palm and sighed. Searing anger at herself started to coil in her gut. This was not her. She never ran, she was not weak. In no way. So, what had happened back there? Now, away from that place, her fear was drowned away by anger and she had a hard time understanding why she had been so pathetically afraid.

Another bout of rumbling thunder made her look to the sky. Dark clouds swarmed together, darkening the heavens with their heavy, rain-filled presence.

"I should get going," she told the rabbit. "You should too." She stretched out a hand and stroked his fluffiness. He leaned into her touch and then darted away. A small chuckle choked its way up her throat, dampening the anger. Whatever had happened to her, she had more pressing matters to attend to. Like getting to the cave before she and the blankets were drenched.

****

Her feet carried her swiftly, still a bit unsteady, but she tried her best to ignore that. When she came near the cave, she stopped. An acrid smell tingled in her nose. The scent of smoke and fire. Swallowing hard, she forced her legs the rest of the way and poked her head inside the cave.

There was the human, Christian, sitting in front of a small fire, rubbing his hands together before spreading his fingers out toward the flames.

Flames. Golden-yellow mouths of searing agony, licking at skin, making it blister and burn. She sucked in a breath and green eyes flew up to capture hers. A smirk widened his lips.

"There you are, I thought you ditched me."

She stared at him and then the fire. It was far too close for her liking.

Chris frowned. "You should come inside, it'll start to rain any second now. I can't believe you were right about that." His palm rose and he waved her inside, making the golden light dance on his skin.

She took a step back. "Fire," she breathed.

"Uhm, yes. I got my lighter going after a few tries." He flashed her a grin. Proud, soft and... warm. "I guess, it will get freezing tonight, like this we'll stay warm without having to cuddle." He stood up and walked over. "Come on, sweetheart."

She took another step back, her heel catching on a rock. The blankets tumbled to the ground as her arms flailed, trying to regain her balance. A hand shot out, wrapping around her upper arm, before she was pulled forward and crashed into his chest. Christian's arms came around her back, steadying her.

"Whoa there. I'm not going to hurt you, what's wrong?"

"Fire," she uttered once more as the wave of memories she had left behind was threatening to crash against her. Drowning her.

"Hey, hey, look at me," Chris said as his palms cupped her face. Her eyes tore away from the fire and found his. "It's okay, it's just fire. Nothing is going to happen to you. I promise."

His eyes were wide with surprise and worry, but there was also something else in them. Truth. He believed in what he had just told her. He believed that nothing was going to happen to her.

"I'll put it out, okay? Just... just stay here and I'll put it out." His hands vanished from her cheeks then rubbed over her shoulders and down her arms in soft, warming circles. Christian stepped back and went into the cave again, no doubt to kill the fire.

"Wait," she said.

He turned around, cocking a brow in question.

"Leave it." She gathered the blankets and stepped into the cave, never letting the fire out of her sight. Still, she wasn't able to go up to it without the fear and that looming wave of memories getting too close. The anger from before flared to life inside her again. This, again, was not her. Fear was a foreign notion, something she crushed. Not something ruling her. Never again.

A tug on the blankets in her arms broke the spell. Chris softly pulled at the load she carried, "May I?"

She nodded and let go. He spread the fur out next to the fire and let a blanket fall onto it before he wrapped one of the blankets around her. "Where did you get these?"

She did not answer.

"I take it you're not a fan of fire," he mused while he pulled the edges of cloth around her front. When she didn't respond, he shrugged and took a seat in front of the fire again.

"For me it's heights," he said, spreading out his fingers once more. So close to the flames, like he was almost touching them.

She hissed softly.

"Terrifies the shit out of me. I freeze up and can't move. Even if I know that nothing can happen, like if there's a railing and stuff. Doesn't matter. I still have these pictures in my head where the railing breaks clean off and I fall. I never fell from anywhere, except from a tree when I was a child, but that wasn't really high. So, I have no idea where this fear comes from, it's just always been there.”

The wind in her back grew colder and soon drops of rain beat against her calves. Stinging droplets of freezing cold. They got more intense and bigger by the second and she shuffled forward.

“It's frustrating when your head knows one thing but there is no way in hell you can convince your body to react accordingly.” He smiled and shook his head, gazing at the flames. His expression was forlorn, like he was not here, but far away. She wondered where he had gone to and took another step.

“Sometimes your body does things you can't control. And that can be scary. It makes it hard to move, to think and impossible to breathe. It's a fear that makes you think you're going to die.” His eyes flashed to hers, capturing them. “I might not understand or know anything about you, but this is something I get. And I promise, you are safe. You can sit here.” He a patted the fur behind him. “And I'll be between you and the fire. You'll still get warm, but it can't reach you. Okay?”

She did not want to be afraid, it galled her that she was, and even more that he knew. That he understood. A human who knew her weakness. It was dangerous and if she was smart, she would push him into the fire and run. Right now. Before he did it to her.

But the lake had saved him. It must have been for a reason, and she would not question the decision by killing Christian. What was more, she did not want to. Even though she did not care for humans, having someone talking to her, answering her with words, was... nice.

She balled up her fists and walked around the fire, as close to the stone-wall as she could, and came up behind Chris. Slowly, she sank down next to him, leaving him between her and the fire.

"There you go. If it gets too much, I'll put it out. You just say the word."

She glared at him, "Stop treating me as you would a child."

He held up his hands, "I'm sorry, I thought–"

She shook her head. "I know. You helped. You can stop now."

Silence fell, only broken by shuffling limbs, the crackling of the fire and Chris feeding the flames with more dry wood. She stared into the golden light as it danced. It was curiously captivating. Flickering and reaching into the air, just like the memories and fear were flickering and reaching for her. The constant view and warmth melted her resolve not to give in. There was no telling what was hidden in her mind, drowned away so long ago.

Searing heat on her skin, her flesh, dozed by dark waters in the night. Screams, laughter, the fire of righteousness in cruel eyes. Merciless.

She sat up straight as a strain of memory pelted through and took a seat deep within her. "I remember," she whispered.

"What?" Chris turned to her. "What did you say?"

"I remember. I had a name. I was... It was Emily. I was called Emily."

Chapter Six

"Emily," her Name felt melodic on his tongue. "Fits you." He scanned her face and those deep eyes that still stared at the flames. She seemed far gone and Chris bet she wasn't even aware she was shivering.

She had a name, and she'd remembered it, plus the fact that she was afraid of fire. Chris wondered what else was hidden away in her mind. Maybe she had experienced something traumatic, which was shut away deeply. Maybe that was the reason she was out here alone and couldn't recall any parents or how she got here.

"Do you remember something else?" Chris asked.

She stared.

"Hello? Emily?" He reached out and nudged her arm.

Her eyes snapped to his hand touching her, but she didn't back away. Emily frowned and her tongue darted out to wet her dry lips. It was both an innocent gesture and a captivating one.

"Why does that happen?" she asked.

Chris pulled his fingers back. "Why does what happen?"

Her face grew dark an instant later as she regarded him with the disgruntled expression he was slowly getting used to. "It does not matter." Emily's gaze bounced along the cave walls to the rain outside. Her nostrils flared slightly and her face relaxed completely. She remained like that for a while, her face tilted up, watching the downpour, ignoring Chris.

"How do I leave?" he asked.

Emily's mouth corners twitched downward. "You do not."

An ice-cold tingle shot through Chris' gut. He swallowed. "You mean...you said I'd die if I went further than the tree. That was a joke, right? There is a way I can leave. There has to be." He was not staying here. Not that the company wasn't top-notch eye-candy, but he had a life to get back to.

The woman at his side hung her head and sighed. "If there is a way, I do not know of it." She got up and strode to the cave entrance. "I know you do not believe. You humans have trouble with what you cannot explain, you even have trouble explaining what you can only feel." Emily turned to him. "If you will, I can show you."

Chris raised a brow. "Show me what?"

"That which one cannot explain, but only experience."

He was intrigued, but he had also witnessed a bunch of fucked up shit since he got here. Chris didn't know if he wanted to broaden his horizon any further. That was before she lifted her dress and pulled it over her head.

He gaped. "What the hell?"

Emily just looked at him, dropping the dress on a blanket. "You can follow, or not. It is your decision," she said before she stepped from the cave.

Chris stared into the dark, he couldn't wrap his head around what just happened. His addled brain hadn't dreamt up anything last night, she was a knock-out. But he was too thunderstruck to even move a muscle. After the initial shock wore off, curiosity snaked its way into his mind. What on earth did she want to show him? Naked? In the rain?

He jumped to his feet and took off his own clothes. They might have a fire, but the night was far from warm. Clad only in his boxers, he followed her.

The rain was heavy now, every few seconds bolts of lightning forked across the sky, followed by deafening thunder. Chris was drenched at once, the drops of water like icy pinpricks of a thousand needles. The mud pressing up between his toes washed away by the rain with each stumbling step forward. He lifted his arm to shield his face somewhat and peered into the night. Another flash of light revealed Emily standing on a ledge a little way down.

Finally, sliding and nearly planting his face into the mud a few times, he reached her side, his teeth chattering, courtesy of the merciless wind. She looked into the distance, in the direction of the lake. Every time lighting struck, it lit up, fuzzy and silver.

"You followed," she said, her voice floating, nearly drowned away.

"Yup." He was very consciously not looking at her, but followed her example and gazed into the distance. At what exactly, he had no idea.

"Close your eyes," Emily said.

His manners forgotten, his eyes snapped to her. "Seriously? I'm standing on a ledge, elevated, barefoot in a fucking storm. And you want me to close my eyes?"

She crinkled her nose, looking like a snarling, wet puppy. "I told you to choose. You have, now close your eyes."

Chris hesitated for a second, but then he let his lids slide shut. He jumped slightly as he felt a small, wet hand take his. Her touch was strange. Cool, yet tingling. Soft, yet firm. And though her hand was tiny in his, he could feel the strength in her grip, and he got the silly notion that if she wanted, she could crush his bones with one squeeze.

"Breathe," she said. "Steady. Smell the rain, hear it, feel it on your skin."

He concentrated on his breathing, on the sound of the storm, on the scent of it, but he was preoccupied mainly with the fact that she was touching him, and the thought that she was very much naked. But after a while his one-lined thoughts dampened and Chris was able to focus on what she had told him.

"Good. Now focus on my hand." Her voice was close, even though he knew she hadn't moved. "Feel my skin against yours. Feel the life in it, the blood pumping in my fingertips."

At first, he wanted to ask if she had lost it, but he didn't dare to. It didn't matter anyway because a second later he *could* feel it. The life she had told him about beat against him, wild, uncontrollable, alive. She seemed to hum with a foreign power. It washed over him, similar to the water from above, just as harsh and real. Goosebumps blanketed his entire body, making him shiver slightly.

"Now slowly open your eyes and stay calm." This time her voice was even closer, it felt almost as if she spoke inside of his head.

Chris took a deep breath to do as she said...and gasped.

The world had changed. The water running down the hill shone. Illuminated blue, glowing silver and shiny green. It ran down in twirling rivulets, its destination the lake. The Lake. It was the source of the light, blinding and breathtaking. Chris squinted, it seemed like the lake was...beating. Slow and deep, like a heart, sending out ripples of that same power he felt beating in Emily's hand. He turned his head and his mouth fell open. She was the same as the lake. Shining like a beacon through the storm, the flashes of lightning not dulling her radiance for even a moment.

"The lake and I are one. Its heart beats within me and mine in its depths. The lake gives life to the land around, the animals, the trees, and the air." She waved her free hand in a semi-circle, encasing everything around them in that gesture.

Chris tore his eyes from her to look. And he could see it. The light suffused everything, fainter than her or the lake, but there. The forest glowed subtly, nearly as far as his eyes could see. But a good distance away, the glow was gone.

"It gives life, but it does not reach indefinitely. The tree you could not pass? That was the edge of it. You should have died, but for some reason the lake healed you." Emily placed her palm on his chest, above his heart. She looked up, rain drops clinging to her lashes, running down her cheeks and pearling over her lips. "Your heart beats to the same rhythm as mine and the lake's. Look."

Chris started hyperventilating when he saw a patch of his skin glow and pulse slightly. Right where the bullet-hole should have been. "What the fuck?" He stumbled back, out of Emily's reach. And the moment they lost their connection everything turned to normal.

"The lake gives you life, but you cannot survive out of its reach. That which it gives, has no power past the line. If you cross it, you will die. Do you understand now?"

****

The human had his arms crossed around his knees, holding onto them for dear life, while his wild eyes stared into nothingness. He chewed his bottom lip with a frenzy and from time to time, he threw her glances. The flickering light of the fire danced across the naked skin of his legs and torso. The sizable muscles in his arms clenched as he held onto himself.

"You glowed," he said.

"I did not glow, I just showed y–"

"The lake glowed," he interrupted. "Every-fucking-thing glowed. I glowed."

There was a nudge in her mind, a long-lost memory akin to his confusion and helplessness, but Emily brushed it off firmly. She'd had about as much musty-old memories as she could stand for one night.

Chris' panicked eyes found hers, their green glinting in the light. "How?"

Emily lowered her face and pushed a small stone across the cave floor with her big toe. "I do not know. It has always been this way. I have always been this way." She drew her brows together. "At least, I think I have." She circled the pebble with her toe, concentrating on the small grating sound it made. She did not want to ponder this topic further.

A movement at the line of her vision made her look up.

Chris was rubbing his head and face furiously with both palms. "Fuck," he grated out. "This isn't real. Can't be. Any moment now I'll wake up."

"If this is a dream," Emily said. "Then I have been sleeping for centuries."

The human was still muttering things to himself, he had obviously not heard her. Since it was mostly nonsensical stuff, Emily let her thoughts wander, forcefully leading them away from the memories threatening to brim her mind. There was something strange about the human. When she had touched him...her skin had tingled. Nothing like that had ever happened before. It was an entirely new feeling. A feeling that pulled at her; beckoning to explore, to understand. A mystery. Emily loved mysteries.

What was more, she had been able to show him. To really show him the lake and herself. The lake was part of him now, and although Emily knew that, she had not been sure it would work. Pity she had not anticipated what it would do to him once he saw it. Humans...weak-minded, the lot of them.

"Okay, okay." He blew out a stream of air though puffed-up cheeks. "Holy shit. Okay." Chris pulled both hands through his wet, tousled hair and looked up. "Explain it to me."

Emily cocked her head to the side, the fear and madness had left his eyes and he watched her expectantly. Not what she had thought he would do, but it was something she could work with.

"It is as I have said, the lake–"

"Yeah, the lake healed me. But what the hell is the lake? It isn't ordinary."

Emily smiled. "It is alive. Even has a consciousness."

Chris snorted. "Yeah, right."

"It does. It is not as quick as yours or mine, but it does perceive things and has a sense of self. Just takes longer to register. That is what I am for. I watch and protect, I wield its power and keep it company."

"You want me to believe that you talk to it?" Chris's eyebrows nearly sprung off his forehead the way he was raising them.

"No. I do not talk to it, do not be ridiculous. But I can feel it, its needs, its secrets and wants. It is as much part of me as I am of it."

The human shook his head. "This is too fucking weird."

"I understand it would come as a shock to one such as you," Emily mused.

"A shock? To one such as me?" Chris rolled his eyes. "Oh, I understand, cause I'm human and you hate those. But tell me, sweet cheeks, if I was able to see what you showed me and the lake healed me, then where did you come from? I doubt the lake just washed you up on the shore one fine day. Maybe something similar happened to you, maybe you are, in fact, as much human as me."

"Me? Human? Now that is just crazy! I am not like your kind." She balled her fists at her sides, reigning in the power that sprang up to aid her should she need it. It vibrated against her knuckles, ready. "Your kind only knows how to take, to defile and destroy. They hunt, kill and ravish everything they come across. That is why I throw them out, that is why I kill them if they come back. Thinking I am the same is just preposterous!"

"You have a very one-sided view on things, you know." He rubbed his temples with his fingers. "Whatever, I'll go to sleep now. Hopefully, I'll wake up in the real world."

He pulled on his shirt and lay down on the fur next to the fire. Turning away from the fire he closed his eyes firmly, ignoring her. Emily watched the flames flicker with a remaining jolt of unease, as she pondered his words. She could not be like him, it was impossible. The life she lived, the differences between what she had seen and experienced of humans and herself were too profound. No, there was no way she was one of them. No way.

Chapter Seven

Chris woke to the most amazing smell ever. He couldn't really place it, had never smelled the combination before. Sweet, like freshly cut grass and honeysuckle, mingled with a spice he didn't know. He cracked a lid and frowned. His nose was buried in a waterfall of gold. *What the…?*

His brain caught up to what he saw and he scooted back a bit. Emily. Her pale red mane was fanned out behind her and he had obviously dipped his face into the tresses. So, she had eventually done what he'd said and laid down next to him, leaving him between her and the fire. It all came back to him then and he groaned softly. He was still here. He hadn't woken to the real world. *What a fucking trip!* Chris shifted to his back and pulled the blanket around him. Emily must have placed the blanket over him, he couldn't remember taking it.

Closing his eyes as firmly as he could, he willed himself back to sleep. He didn't want this new reality. It sucked. Lakes and women glowing, his skin doing the same freaky shit... No, he was so trying again with the whole waking-in-the-real-world business.

****

Chris didn't know if minutes or hours had passed when he opened his eyes once more. He sat up to an empty cave. The fire had died but the coals still radiated warmth. Chris grimaced as he patted the cave-floor to his left for his clothes. Seemed like sleeping hadn't worked – he was still here. He looked to the side, opening and closing his mouth to lose the taste of sleep, and his eyes snapped open. His clothes were gone. As were his shoes. He rummaged around, lifted the blankets, no clothes or shoes, only his broken phone and lighter. *Had Emily taken the rest?*

Chris stood and looked down his body, his feet and legs were caked in dried mud, he'd been so out of it last night he hadn't even noticed, or cared. He walked to the cave entrance and stopped short when he saw something drawn into the sand before it. It looked like a child's drawing, showing a line of trees and the lake. A stick-figure with long hair stood on the banks of the lake. *Why hadn't she just written him a message? Could she even read or write?*

He huffed out a breath and began making his way down. Chris soon discovered that wearing shoes all the time had made his feet soft and sensitive. The coarse sand felt like sandpaper rubbing against his soles after a time and the tiny stones he overlooked were a bitch. Cursing all the way, he stalked down the hill feeling like a comic figure. *Why the hell had she taken his shoes?* One didn't just take a guy's shoes from him, or his pants for that matter. He sighed in relief once his feet met grass. Soft, cool grass. He stopped and just enjoyed the feel for a second, then continued on his way.

Hoping he was going in the right direction, he picked the left side of the lake. Since it was huge, Emily could be anywhere. Chris was fairly sure she would be on the bank she had brought him to on the night they met. Thing was, he wasn't sure where that was.

Chris felt as if someone was watching him and looked around. Not far from him, a rabbit with one straight and one bent ear watched him. "What?" Chris asked.

The rabbit scratched behind his ear with his hind paw, never taking its beady eyes from Chris.

"You wouldn't know where to find Emily?" Chris asked, grinning at the little guy. The rabbit stopped the scratching and hopped a few feet away. Chris snorted, but followed him, sure any second the little ball of fluff would take off zig-zagging through the forest. The rabbit looked over and hopped away again, making his little white tail appear and vanish, like a homing beacon. Feeling like a total idiot, Chris trailed him, curios as to where it would lead him. Most likely a burrow.

After a few minutes, the lake came into view through the trees, sparkling in the morning sun. Enticing. Rationally, Chris wanted to stay away from it as far as he could after what he'd seen, but there was a subtle pull toward it coming from his belly. A need to touch it, or even take a dip.

The rabbit stopped between two large trees and looked at Chris expectantly. Squinting against the sun and lake, Chris came to stand next to it. A breath he hadn't known he'd held escaped his lungs. There was the lake, spread out in all its glory, and on the pebbled bank was Emily. Dancing.

Chris looked at the rabbit, but the little guy was already gone. What the hell had just happened? He'd asked a friggin rabbit for directions, and it had worked? *Was he turning into some kind of Fairytale Princess?*

The cold fingers of panic caressed his mind softly but before he could freak out, his eyes landed on Emily again. Her white dress was wet at the seam and water drops flew everywhere whenever she turned and twirled. Her hair fanned out in the wind, her feet skipped across the bank into the water and her arms twisted and fluttered gracefully. She looked completely crazy, and happy. The smile on her face was nothing short of blinding. It was a happiness he didn't know, had never even come close to. He felt himself wishing he knew that abandoned elation radiating from Emily. Even just a bit of it would be more than he'd ever known. Not that he was unhappy. He liked the thrill of conning, never knowing if and when you would get caught. But it was something fleeting, a high from the moment. What he was seeing a few feet away was different. That happiness went soul deep.

With one sweep of the view before him, his panic was flung from his mind, in its stead, a smile crept onto his lips. He stumbled down the bank, cursing when his feet hit the pebbles and hobbled on until his soles reached the cool mud. Then his skin touched the water and a shiver pranced across his back. The good kind.

"Christian?" Emily squealed, apparently surprised by his sudden appearance.

"You drew me a picture, remember? Here I am."

She laughed. Her face reddening and her arms circling her belly she doubled over. "You...you looked like...like a kitten stalking through water."

Chris scowled at her. "If someone wouldn't have taken my shoes, I wouldn't have blisters and cuts on my soles."

Emily just giggled. "They were too loud, you do not need them. Besides, you will soon get used to it."

"I don't want to get used to it. I want my goddamned shoes!"

The crazy woman pursed her lips, trying hard not to laugh. She lost a second later.

"Oh, so that's how you want to play it?" Chris asked and lunged at her.

Emily yelped and danced out of his reach. She circled him with baffling speed and nudged his side. "Boop!"

"What the hell? Emily, I want my shoes, now! Come on, stand still."

She laughed and circled him once more, this time she tapped his shoulder. "Boop!"

Chris found it hard to stay angry, her cheerful face and the sheer joy with which she evaded and dodged him was a strange combination of innocence and sensuality. It had begun as all play, but along the way it turned to something else. Coaxing him to chase her, mixed with sidelong glances and subtle lip bites heated his blood. Chris was sure she had no idea what she was doing, it was subconscious, but there. Her eyes flashed across his body curiously, lingering here and there, as if she was chasing him and not the other way around.

Bit by bit, he analyzed her movements and began to anticipate them. Her arm shot out to 'boop' him and Chris grabbed hold of her wrist. Squealing and laughing they tumbled into the lake. Spluttering they both emerged and Chris pulled Emily closer. "You give up?"

She grinned at him. "Never."

Chris dunked her and she dove away, slipping from his grasp. "Em? Emily?" He watched the water around him but the sun reflected in such a way that he couldn't see a thing. Hands grabbed his ankles and his feet were pulled out from under him. Emily shot up, wound her arms around his shoulders and pressed him down.

Shaking his head, he came up again. "Oh, now you're just asking for it."

Their game of dunking and chasing lasted for some time, during which Chris laughed until his belly hurt and his breath became ragged. He hadn't had this much fun in a long time. He did have a hard time combining this version of her with the one he'd gotten to know before. But after a while, he just enjoyed their game. She was fast and a lot stronger than she looked, but he got her several times and always chuckled at her disgruntled expression, she wasn't used to losing.

****

"So, are you going to tell me where my stuff is?" Chris asked after they had finally settled down. They sat on the bank, drying in the sun, their chests still heaving.

"I washed your clothes, they are on the stones over there," she said pointing to a collection of rocks not far away. "But your shoes... You should really consider letting them go. You cannot feel with them on."

"What the hell is that supposed to mean?"

Emily sighed and shook some hair off her shoulders. "Skin connects you to the lake, to the forest, and your feet can feel that connection." She opened one eye and glanced at him. "Want me to show you?"

Chris dug his elbows further into the ground on either side and leaned back. "No. You showed me plenty last night. I'm still trying to wrap my head around that. I should be focusing on a way to get out of here."

"It is not so bad here."

Chris couldn't be sure of her words, they had been little more than a whisper and when he looked over she had closed her eyes. "Thank you. For washing my stuff, I could have done it myself."

"I know. Next time you will. Plus my dress, of course. Something for something."

A smile stole itself onto his lips. "Of course."

Emily sat up. "Are you hungry?"

Chris nodded. "I wouldn't mind one or two of those mushrooms. Do you have meat? We could grill something."

62

"I sometimes eat fish," she said. "They overpopulate fast and the predatory fish have trouble regulating, so I help."

"Do they need help now?" Chris asked.

Emily scrunched up her nose, placed one toe into the water and concentrated. "One or two schools have too many fish. I'll get them so we can what was it girl them?"

"*Grill*," Chris said. "We'll roast them over fire."

Her eyes widened. "I will not waste life so you can burn it."

He had to chuckle. "We're not going to burn it, just roast. Trust me, it'll taste great."

"Fine, but if I do not like it, you will wash my dress forever."

"Deal." Chris smiled and stretched out his palm. Emily watched it and pulled a brow up. "You shake it."

Emily circled his wrist with two fingers and shook his hand. "Why?"

Chris laughed and took her hand in his. "No, like this." He shook her hand. "It's like a promise made between two people. A deal."

She captured his gaze with hers. "Deal."

****

Emily slipped off her dried dress and waded into the deep after Chris had left to get his fire maker. She had no idea if she would like what he was promising, but if she did not, she would have time to do other things while he washed her dress. She smiled and swam out. The human was playful, granted, she had coaxed him to be, but it had been nice. Nice to laugh with someone who could laugh back. And the touching was...nice in a strange way. There had been that humming again, which she did not understand. Maybe he knew what it was about. Since she had shown him last night, she felt different about him. Emily was sure now that it had been no accident, the lake had chosen him for some reason.

She grew curious about him. He was so different from her, had different secrets, and she felt she wanted to know them. If the lake deemed him worthy, then maybe he was safe. Maybe she could trust him with her secrets in return.

The water was cool around her, the sun hot. The mix of the two was tickling her skin and she smiled. Emily stopped and floated on the spot, she twirled the power of the lake around her fingers and waited until she felt the fish. She curled her fingers and pulled, then she waited. A few minutes passed while she tread water and pulled on the connection. A thrumming went through her fingers and a fish came swimming her way, lured and pulled from its school.

She stroked his soft and sleek body while he circled her. "Will you do me the honor?" He swam into her outstretched hands and she lifted him from the water. Emily placed her lips to his gaping ones and tugged on the power within him. The fish grew still, sleeping before the life left him. "Thank you, my friend." If she was not mistaken, she had watched this one hatch a year ago. Emily was rarely wrong. Cradling the fish close to her chest, she swam back.

Stepping from the water, she deemed herself too wet to bother with her dress just yet. Passing it by, she walked up the small hill where she could make out Chris. He had lit a fire and was busy with some sticks.

"What is that for?" Emily asked, stepping closer.

His eyes flew up and he gaped, before turning away from her quickly. "Jesus, woman! Why are you always naked?"

"Why are you not?" she retorted. Emily shrugged when he did not answer, she placed the fish on the grass next to the fire and pranced down the hill to get dressed.

She grinned as the wind fanned across her skin, drying it. Spinning in circles, she sent pebbles flying in every direction. The melody of the small waves made her hum a song with it as she picked up her dress and pulled it on. Clapping her hands to the song and swaying to it, she strutted back up the hill.

"Better?" she asked, dropping down next to Chris. He just nodded, busy with gutting the fish. When he was done, he speared the fish on a stick and hung the stick between two sticks on either side of the fire. Emily watched as he turned the fish, looking everywhere but her. She sighed and got up, took the innards and carried them to the treeline. There was a fox burrow nearby, and the little ones would love something different.

Sitting down, she continued her vigil. He was new. That had to be it, she was watching his every move because she was not used to a human this close. Curiosity, pure and simple. And humming skin where he touched. Chris had pulled on his pants but not his shirt and something foreign in Emily was pleased at that. At being able to ogle so much of the humming skin.

Chapter Eight

The fish tasted delicious. It melted in her mouth, heated goodness making her taste buds relish every bite she took.

"You like it," Chris assessed with a smirk as he watched Emily gobble up her share.

"Mh hm," was all the answer she gave him.

Emily closed her eyes and tilted her face into the soft breeze, enjoying the taste on her tongue mixed with the scents around her. The heat from the fire next to them still reached her, even though she had taken up Christian's offer to put him between her and the flames once again. She realized that with him shielding her from it, the prodding of those memories and the fear twisting her heart was bearable.

"So, what is it you do all day out here anyway?" Chris asked, capturing her attention and drawing her away from her inner ruminations.

Emily swallowed her current bite and glanced at him. "I watch, go for swims, help those who need it and...well, I live."

He frowned at that, clearly those weren't the answers he had been expecting. "What do you watch and who needs your help? There aren't any people around." Confusion shone from his face as he poked the gleaming coals with one of the sticks he had used to roast the fish.

"I watch *everything*. The wind making patterns on the water, the animals around us, I listen to the song of their voices and the beatings of their hearts. There is a doe who will be giving birth in a few days, and if she needs it, I will help her get through it." Emily cocked her head to the side. "What do you do all day?"

The confusion had not left his face, and while he thought on her question, his expression scrunched up even further. The way his lips twisted and the skin of his nose crinkled made Emily smile. She had never seen a face as expressive as his.

"I...uh..." He shook his head and prodded the fire some more. "I guess you could say I travel a lot. I have been to many places and met a huge amount of people. I read them to find their weaknesses."

"What for would you need to know their weaknesses?"

He shrugged and looked away. Emily waited, nibbling on the rest of her meal.

"It's hard to explain." He cleared his throat.

"I am not stupid, I am sure if you tried explaining, I would understand."

"I'm not doubting that," Chris said, still avoiding her eyes.

It dawned on Emily then. "You do not wish to explain. Why is that?"

His head swiveled around until their eyes met. "The reason behind it isn't...decent."

"Humans are not decent, why should you be any different?"

Chris snorted. "Yeah, I forgot, your opinion of 'humans' isn't that flattering." He sighed and threw the stick into the fire, making an array of sparks erupt and shoot skyward. "I steal, okay? It's what I do. I read people to trick them into giving me what I want."

"And what do you want?"

"Money, mostly. To buy food, a bed for the night and stuff."

Emily worried her lower lip for a second. "Buy?"

Chris raised a brow. "Like trading. Money for goods."

She nodded, still a bit unsure. "So...you steal to get something you need to survive. What of the people you steal from? How do they survive?"

"By working for their money. Or by stealing it from those who do," he murmured.

Emily pondered his words for a bit, money and stealing was a foreign concept to her and something she was not sure she understood. "Taking something someone needs and not gifting something in return is not right," she finally said.

A mirthless chuckle escaped Chris. "I told you it wasn't decent."

"You did."

"Can we talk about something else?" he asked, pulling a hand through his tousled hair.

Emily picked at some dirt beneath one of her nails. "We do not have to talk at all, if you rather would not."

"I do, actually. You always say the weirdest things." He smiled at her. "The stuff with listening to hearts?" He shook his head. "So random."

"But I do, if you close your eyes and just listen, you can hear and everything happening around you."

His smile turned indulgent, making a flame of annoyance dance to life inside her. She glowered at him. "Just because you neither believe, nor listen, does not mean what I say is untrue. Your ignorance is not my problem. It does not mean that I am insane, or that I will tolerate you viewing me as such."

Emily sprang up and stalked away. It took only a second before she could hear him jogging her way to catch up. "Em, I'm sorry. It's just – will you please stop and let me explain?"

She pivoted around and crashed face-first into his oncoming chest. Jumping back and stumbling as she went, he caught her before she fell. His hand that had snatched her elbow with lightning speed flustered her, as it, again, made her skin tingle. She yanked her arm from his hold and stared him down. "I do not like being belittled."

"You know, that is pretty rich coming from you," he said. "You have, in so many words, told me you are better than me since we met."

Emily rolled her eyes, but had to admit he was right. She crossed her arms over her chest and jerked her chin up. "Explain then."

Chris let his gaze dart to the side and over the lake, his lips quirking into a small smile before they turned into a thin line and he frowned. "Since I woke up to meet you, I keep on thinking I'll wake from the strangest dream ever. Being here? Seeing what you have shown me yesterday? Being shot at without having a wound? Not to mention not being able to leave past a certain tree?" He spread his hands in a helpless gesture. "Everything, from you, to all these experiences, is hard to understand, hard to believe. In my world stuff like this doesn't exist. If I ever told anyone about it, I'd be carted off to the nearest asylum."

Though she did not know what an asylum was supposed to be, Emily understood what he was trying to tell her.

"I'm sorry if I have offended you, and given what I have seen so far...heck, it's likely that you can sense everything you say you can."

Emily gave him a small nod. "I am sorry too," she forced herself to say. "For belittling you. The humans I have encountered so far have been cruel and evil beings. The lake healed you, it does not act without reason. From what I have seen so far, I also believe you to be different from the rest."

Chris was staring at her, making Emily feel slightly self-conscious after a while. He blinked in quick succession and then gathered his breath for an answer. "I'm not...I told you a minute ago what I do for a living."

"You have. But you neither tried to kill nor hurt me. That alone makes you different."

His eyes widened. "Why would someone try to hurt you?"

Emily opened her mouth as a wave of memory threatened to drown her at thinking about it. "They defiled my lake, so I fought them. Before that...I cannot remember." Her brows knit together. "It is all fuzzy. Yesterday, I remembered my name, and a night of flames and pain. I...do not want to think on it any longer." Emily looked down and rubbed her arms, suddenly feeling a chill creep over her body despite the warm sun.

"Hey," Chris said and reached out a palm to squeeze her shoulder. Emily watched his hand on her and there it was again, that strange buzz, chasing away the chill she had felt a moment ago.

"Why does that happen?" she asked.

"Why does what happen?" Chris asked.

"When we touch, it feels strange. It tingles and hums over my skin, like goosebumps. Pleasant ones. Is that normal if humans touch?" She looked up to meet his gaze and saw his Adam's apple bobbing as he swallowed.

Chris tugged back his hand and Emily felt a sinking sensation in her stomach. Like a loss.

"Sometimes," he murmured. He smiled and stepped away. "You up for a swim?"

Emily narrowed her eyes, it was evident he didn't want to linger on the subject, but she would never say no to a swim in her lake. "Of course."

"Race you to the shore," Chris shouted and sprinted off.

Still a little wary, but infected by the enthusiasm in his voice, she gave chase.

The human ripped off his shirt, it fluttered to the ground before he stumbled out of his pants, nearly planting his nose into the pebbled ground in the process. Emily giggled at the sight but stopped short when he lunged into the water and her feet touched the edge of the lake, her hands gripping the edges of her dress. Uncertain.

Huffing and shaking his hair out, Chris came up grinning. "What are you waiting for?"

"You always seem to dislike my nakedness, but I—"

"I'll just turn around until you're in the water." He did just that and with a rustling of cloth, her dress pooled at her feet. She stepped from it and followed him, a foreign feeling manifesting itself right below her chest. Never having felt it before, Emily struggled to come up with what exactly it was she was feeling.

"And by the way, I don't dislike your nakedness. At all. It's just that...where I come from, it's not right to see another person like that." His palms skimmed over the small waves rippling around his body, while Emily walked up to him. "Not if you're not...shit...I'm bad at this. You know what? Never mind. You can be naked as much as you want, it's me who isn't used to it. I'll deal with it, okay?"

Emily came to stand next to him and nodded when his head turned her way. The soft lapping of the waves tickled her belly and she smiled. Little kisses from her lake. She crouched down and kicked off, darting through the coolness, feeling the comfortable sluggishness her limbs had to fight against surround her. This was it. This was what she lived for.

Weightless, she shot through the coolness, leaving Chris behind in a few heartbeats. He was a good swimmer and could nearly keep up. For a while. Emily smiled and slowed until he swam at her side.

"You're like a damn fish," he spluttered.

"I do have a lot of practice," Emily conceded.

"I bet."

Swimming beside each other in silence for a while, Emily felt at peace. Not only was she inside her beloved lake, but she was not alone. Not that she ever was alone, there was so much life around her, and she felt connected to all of it. But Chris was different. He could acknowledge her to a degree animals could not. He laughed, talked, and entertained her in a whole different way. Even the silent companionship of sharing a swim was...nice.

He was a mystery, a puzzle, occupying her mind. She never knew what he would do or say next. That alone was exhilarating.

Emily concentrated on the feel of her body, the straining of her muscles with every stroke. The way her arms, legs, and breath got heavy after a while. Almost painful, but in a soft, warm, soothing way.

When they had nearly reached the other bank, she stopped to turn around.

"What is that?" Chris asked, treading water and pointing at one of the black, wooden beams from the abandoned settlement. It poked out over a few smaller trees, which hid the burnt and broken houses from view.

"Nothing," Emily mumbled and shot off. She should not have swum this far.

The human had not moved. "It's not nothing, let's go check it out."

"No."

Chris turned and raised a brow. "Why not?"

"Because I do not want to."

His head turned back to face the beam. "It looks human made."

"Because it is." Emily rolled her eyes and continued on her way.

"Would you stop? You know what's there, don't you?"

She slowed down and sighed at his curious face. "Yes, I do. And I am telling you, it is nothing."

Chris shrugged, an impish grin widening on his face. "If it's 'nothing' then you won't mind if I went and checked it out." He started off in the direction, throwing a "you coming?" over his shoulder.

Emily ground her teeth, so much for nice companionship. The inner debate about what to do lasted for about three seconds. Grumbling beneath her breath she followed the insolent human.

****

Chris felt the ground, slick and squishy under his feet soon and walked up the bank, smirking when he heard Emily grumbling and huffing behind him. He began to enjoy annoying her. It was damned easy to push her buttons.

Without waiting for her, he continued on, cursing loudly at the pebbles which poked and nicked his soles. He huffed out a breath when he stepped on soft, cool grass and walked past the small trees, obscuring his view of what lay beyond.

Rounding a couple of bushes, he stopped short at what he saw. A collection of ruins and an old dust road nearly completely overgrown greeted his eyes. The huts looked old, some burnt and all of them crumbling under the weight of time. One house, bigger than the rest, sat in the middle and was the only one with all four walls halfway in order.

"This was a settlement," he said as he heard footsteps behind him. When he didn't get an answer, he turned to Emily. She stood there, stark-naked, with frightened eyes, scanning the scene. Her breath came in shallow bursts and she knotted her fingers until her knuckles became white. She swallowed once, twice, and started shaking.

Chris walked over. "Em? Emily? What's wrong?" He stretched out his hand when she continued staring without acknowledging him, but pulled it back before he touched her. Her eyes snapped to his and he started when he saw the horror in them. Her terrified gaze held him, while tremor after tremor shook her body.

"Flames, burning flesh, pain. They are coming. They are coming for the witch. To burn and drown her. They are coming. They..."

"Emily! What's wrong? Who is coming?" Her horrified eyes seared straight into his mind, freaking him out.

"They come with steel and fire, to burn, to rip apart, to kill. They are COMING!" Shrieking like a banshee she clawed at her arms, knotting her fingers into her hair and pulling.

Chris couldn't take it any longer and grabbed hold of her, folding his arms around her. With an ear splintering wail, she scratched at his hands, arms, back, anywhere she could reach.

"It's okay. I got you. Shhh..."

She wriggled and fought, still screaming until sobs took over her trembling body and she sagged against him. "They are coming. They are coming to kill me."

"No one is gonna kill you. Shhh. I'm here, Em. I'm here. Calm down, sweetheart."

She sobbed and cried out, shivering in his arms, making his heart swell with pain at seeing hers. "I do not want to be here when they come...I cannot...I–"

"It's okay. We'll leave. Right now." He bent down slinging an arm under her knees, so she folded to his chest. Chris picked her trembling body up and left as fast as he could. He picked the fastest route to the opposing bank he could map out from what he had seen from this place so far. Emily cried and shook the whole way while whispering things from time to time, which made an icy breath of fear blow over his back.

Chapter Nine

Fingers grabbed her, belonging to hands made strong and rough by a hard life. Her slender wrists bruised from the pressure they dealt. Her kicking feet not finding their mark, but after her teeth pierced skin and bit down, a hand came sailing, knocking back her head, making it swim. Her fighting body was hauled away, dragged through a dark night split by torches that lit up hateful faces and condemning eyes around her. Smoke tingled in her nose and she knew where they were headed. Her panicked screams pierced the night.

Fire. Licking up her skin hungrily, roaring for more. Yells and cheers from countless mouths. Their chanting mixing and drowning her unanswered cries. Her screams for mercy yielding to nothing but her voice slowly fading, scratching in her scorching throat.

"Burn the witch! Burn the whore of Satan!"

Manic eyes, widely ripped open, putting the white on display, danced up and down at the edges of her vision. Eyes belonging to foreign faces – no. She knew these faces. Each and every one of them. She did, did she not? Cannot be sure. Too much pain to think.

The agony. It was everything she knew as her skin and flesh fell prey to the flames. As blisters grew until they burst making the fire hiss each time they did. The scent of burning meat and hair causing her coarse throat to flex, trying to gag. Her limbs shook and jerked as they were consumed, useless to help her. She could not see, could not feel anything except for the roaring burn. The pain grew until it was unbearable, then it doubled. A last, hoarse, yelp left her roasted lips, after which darkness descended on her like a merciful blanket.

In the far distance a voice rose from the chanting and sizzling of flames. Clear, fearful and determined. "Emily!"

"Emily."

"Emily, wake up!" Strong fingers pressed into her shoulders, her skin. *Wait a second! Her skin? It was charred, useless, gone. Why was she –* Emily opened her eyes, a wail on her lips, and came face to face with Chris, his forest-green eyes wide and shocked. His gaze ground her in the moment. *A dream, it had all been a dream. Thank the lake! Too real.*

Emily knew, way in the back of her horrified mind, it had been more than a dream. However, she chose to ignore it for the time being as, for a second, tears of utter relief sprang to her eyes. She sobbed uncontrollably, relishing the feel of her cool, unmarred skin, the clean air she was breathing. But still her heart hammered, threatening to explode in her chest and she could not push back the acute panic which had gripped her only moments ago. Her hands fluttered and trembled up and down her arms. She needed to feel herself whole. All the while sobs raked her, seemingly unending.

Suddenly a set of arms encircled Emily, hugging her to a broad warm body. She jerked in Christian's hold with dim surprise, her mind too wrapped up in itself to really register what was happening. The warmth around her was soft, the pressure of his hug gentle, nonthreatening, and a dam inside Emily broke. She had cried before, now she bawled, burying her face into his muscular chest. It was as if the warmth of his body seeped into her, stretching out her chest, making her heart ache even more. But his warmth also made it bearable.

Emily's tears found no end. The moment Chris had touched her, it had been over. The ice blocks inside her, built up to protect, thawed and nourished her tears.

His hands ran over her back and he gently swayed them both from side to side. His deep voice murmured nonsensical stuff into her ear, but its sound was soothing. Her hands shot out around him and she could feel him jump as her nails sank into his back, clutching him closer, holding onto him for dear life. She could not remember the last time she had been held, not like this anyhow. Never like this. The only human hands touching her had always been rough, bruising, intending to hurt.

After clawing at Christian's back for some time, Emily's panic started to dim. His soothing voice, the rocking and the warmth seeping into her were all the things she could focus on. He shifted in her hold, so her head rested on his shoulder and their chests pressed against each other. Emily felt his steady heartbeat thrum next to her erratic one. She squeezed her eyes shut, making a bout of tears stream down her cheeks and into his shirt. Fighting the hiccups from her crying, Emily concentrated. She listened to his heart and gradually the pace of her own slowed, until it was almost in sync with his.

Chris stroked her hair carefully and pulled back a little so he could look at her. "Better?"

All she could muster was a nod, the corners of her mouth trembling with a failed smile. Emily drew in a huge, hiccupy breath and the moment her tears had dried, a wave of tiredness overtook her. She rubbed at her swollen eyes, barely able to keep them open.

"You can lie down if you want," Chris told her, his voice a low rumble. He scooted away from her, giving her some space.

A sudden jolt of panic had her hands shooting out for him. He halted and smiled softly, it was not pity, but understanding shimmering in his eyes. Still, Emily felt stupid for her weak body betraying her like that. Like she needed him, like she did not want him to go. She forced her hands back down and with it, the panic she felt at being cold and alone again.

Chris plucked a blanket up from behind him and draped it over her, then he lay down next to her. Emily watched him all the while, until he spread his arms, inviting her in.

"I'm not going anywhere," he said.

Emily warred with herself for all of two seconds. His warmth was too good to give up. And he had carried her here, back to the cave, so maybe she could trust him. Trust him enough to let him close. Trust him enough to warm her freezing insides against him.

She released a shaky breath and let him pull her in his arms. Her head found a comfortable space on his broad chest while both his arms slid around her, holding her.

They just lay there for long moments and Emily concentrated on Christian to flee her frantic mind. On his smell, his rising and sinking chest, the way his hands stroked her shoulders from time to time. This was nice, just being held. She frowned, knowing she was lying to herself. This was not nice, it was incredible. And if she wasn't cautious, it could become addictive.

"Do you want to talk about it?" his deep voice was soft and non-threatening.

Did she? Emily was not sure. On the one hand, she did not want to relive her dream. On the other hand, she knew talking helped. She had never had anyone answer to her ramblings before, but just saying the words had always helped her if there had been something she had not understood. Or if it had been something she grieved about. Like the time her bear friend had died. She had told every animal around about her, had even talked to the lake. It had helped.

But nobody answering was the point. What if she told Chris and he did not understand? What if he did not look at her with that small smile anymore? A smile that told her he thought she was a bit crazy but could not help himself to smile anyway.

"I do not know," she told him.

"If you're uncomfortable about it, we could start small. Has something like this happened to you before?"

Emily swallowed past the fear in her throat. "I... I do not remember. It could have... no. I do not think so."

Chris played with a strand of her hair, stroking it from her shoulder then picking it up between two fingers. "It didn't seem like a dream, normally people sleep during those."

A shiver shook her body and she felt his arms tighten around her. "I know it was not a dream," she said. "Being near the settlement always makes me feel dread. But not like this. Yesterday, I was there as well and something happened." Emily swallowed. "I remembered pain and my name."

"So, you think it was a memory?"

Emily nearly did not dare, but her head nodded a fraction. She did not want, whatever she was battling with, to be a memory. Had it been a dream, it would have been fine, but knowing she truly lived through fire...

"How did I forget?" she whispered. Her breath picked up, same as her heartbeat, while her skin tingled all over and constricting pain rose in her chest. Flashes of hot and cold washed over her in waves and every hair she had on her body stood to attention, trying to stem the tide as her mind was warring with her body. After a few seconds, her erratic breath did not get past the knot of panic in her throat and Emily gasped, clawing at her neck.

"Em! Emily, look at me," Chris said and palmed her face with both hands, directing her gaze at him. "Now breathe with me, do what I do."

Emily stared at his green eyes without blinking, frozen in place. She tried to suck in a lungful of air, but nothing happened.

Chris grabbed one of her frantic, scratching hands and pressed the palm to his chest. "Do what I do, Em," he told her again. Her hand shook against him, trembling like the wings of a bumblebee. His chest expanded, strong, steadfast, and warm. Her palm followed the movement as he exhaled and, without knowing how, she mirrored him.

"There you go," he mumbled. "And another one."

For long moments, they breathed together while Emily concentrated solely on not concentrating at all. Sinking ever deeper into the sight of him a thought hit her out of nowhere. A thought that rattled everything she thought she knew, a thought so scary her mind jumped back from it in shock.

"What?" he asked. "What did you just think about?"

Emily shook her head as anger surged to the forefront of her mind. This was *not* her. She did not need warm embraces, the company of a human, or his questions. She had lived alone, and well, for years. This quivering, blubbering mess? It was not her!

She pushed herself up, disentangling her body from Christian's' in the process. Wrapping a blanket around her, she wobbled to the cave entrance on unsure feet.

"Em? What's wrong? Where are you going?"

"None of your business," she bit out and stormed from the cave. Her steps became surer with each one she took. Filling her lungs with large bouts of air, she raced down the mountain. The edges of her blanket hooked on bushes and rocks, bits of it ripping in the process. She did not care. Tears, this time angry ones, slid down her cheeks, icing a path along her face, down to her chin, only to fall into oblivion. With quick strokes, she wiped them away to fight the blurriness they brought.

But it didn't matter how fast, or how far she ran, the thought, the dream and the fear did not budge. Not only that, regret, sharp and piercing, nettled up her chest. The way she had treated Chris just now... Abhorrent. He had carried her away from that place, he had been there for her, breathed with her and she...

Emily stopped. She was in a cove where the lake was fed by a small waterfall. Beauty was all around her here. The green of the trees, moss and grass was a blinding shade of lime. Birds sang their little hearts out, complementing the splashing and gargling of the waterfall. Had her heart been in her chest, as opposed to somewhere close to her stomach, she would have sung along. As it was, the beauty was lost to her and she stepped on a stone which reached out over the water. Heavy to her very bones, Emily sat down, letting her feet skim over the veil of water.

But even touching her beloved lake did nothing to stem the cold loneliness she felt. The anger at herself was still gnawing away inside, but it was laced with deep-seated regret. Chris had not deserved her storming off like that, he had not even deserved to have to witness her breakdown. Shame burned up her neck, settling in her cheeks. Weak. She had been so weak.

"What should I do?" she whispered to the lake. "What is happening to me? Why did you–" She swallowed. "Why did you heal him, only to have him stuck here with me?"

As always, no answer came. The lake just kept caressing her feet, all velvet coolness and silver ripples.

As much as she hated herself for it, Emily couldn't help the tears streaming down her face, yet again, as fear grabbed her with its icy fingers. If it truly had been a memory, how come she had forgotten it? And what about before? Who, or what, had she been?

Emily lifted her head and gazed across the lake, her lips quivering as she voiced the question that had frozen her. The question that had made her come here in the first place. "Who am I? *What* am I??" She swallowed, her voice turning to a frightened whisper, "What if who I was changes who I am?"

Chapter Ten

Chris stood at the cave entrance, staring in the direction Emily had left. She was long gone and he didn't know whether to follow or give in to the swell of anger bubbling in his lower belly. Why had she lashed out at him like that? He had only been trying to help. And he had carried her up here, held her, helped her stem a panic-attack and… And she had gone and snapped at him, before racing off to who knew where. What was going on in that strange, beautiful head of hers? Did she need him to follow? He snorted. Well, she could need him all she wanted, but he was staying put. Or was he?

Warring with himself, he stood, noticing a small bird flit up the hill and dive into the thicket of leaves of a tree to his left. Seconds later, the bird shot out once more, only to zap back a few moments later, grass in his beak. As the bird repeated this a few more times, Chris decided to distract his annoyance and – yes – anger at Emily, by sneaking closer to the tree. What was that little guy doing?

Finally, Chris sank down next to the roots of the tree and glanced up into the overwhelming network of branches, twigs, and leaves. Narrowing his eyes, he scanned the canopy, until he saw him. A cute, halfway-done nest sat in the fork of a branch. The bird hung from a twig nearby and wove his newest blade of grass expertly through the nest, adding to the outer wall. Above him, a bird of the same kind – but not as colorful – sat and watched. She chirped and dipped her head to this side and that, clearly monitoring his every move.

Chris felt a smile creep to his lips as he beheld the life before him unfolding. They looked like newlyweds, moving into their first home.

The bubbling anger in his belly simmered down and worry rose. Whatever she had remembered, it seemed like some sort of flashback, maybe she had a form of PTSD. There was no way she was okay. Not after the extent of pain and terror he had witnessed in her eyes, her trembling, and her screams. How long had she been out here, alone? And what about those inexplicable things that kept happening since he got here? Part of him still refused to believe any of it. In fact, he still felt like all of it had to be a dream, no matter what he'd told Emily about trying to believe or understand. He understood nothing, about any of it. And that scared him.

With a shuddering breath, he focused on the tree stem next to him. Maybe he could just go on floating for a little while. Concentrating on her to avoid thinking. As he had done so far. But she had left, and Chris had no idea whereto. A jolt of renewed annoyance at her behavior pierced him and he frowned. Now, he was forced to think, with nothing to focus on but his surroundings – all of which reminded him of how he supposedly couldn't leave.

He picked at the bark of the tree, loosening a piece, then let his palm run over the roughness. A flutter, soft as a butterfly wing, beat against the inside of his palm and he jerked his hand away. "What the hell?" he murmured, inspecting the part of tree bark he had just touched. There was nothing there. Slowly, he extended his hand once more and sure enough, the moment his palm met the bark, another thrum went through his skin. Like a pulse. Soft, warm, prickling.

Hissing, Chris pulled back again, cold fear sweeping him up. "Shit." He jumped to his feet, making the birds above flit from their new nest, whistling their displeasure, but Chris was too stunned to care. On unsure feet, he stumbled from underneath the tree and down the hill. None of this could be real. He needed to get away from all this weirdness. He needed out. The further down he got, the faster his strides got and soon he was flat-out sprinting, not caring that his naked feet got pinched and scraped on the stones.

With his heart beating fast, while he slipped and stumbled to keep his pace, he reached the forest and ran on. The fear inside his chest steadily grew, chasing his frantic breaths and nipping at his bruised heels.

This is a dream. Chris told himself that over and over again, but it didn't slow his running feet, or fought off the panic closing in on him. He had *not* just felt the tree. Alive and beating under his fingers. *No way.* "Wake up," he ground out. "Wake the fuck up!"

Twigs and branches caught hold of his shirt and ripped holes into it. For a second, the thought of him breaking free of this place and stumbling back into society looking like a shredded hobo came into his mind and he laughed hysterically.

Pumping his arms for more speed, he kept going, leaving more distance between him and the lake with each step. But suddenly his movements slowed and dull, throbbing pain crept into his ribcage.

"No. No, no, no. I am leaving. Right now." Chris put more effort into his sprint, feeling like his body would give out from the strain at any moment. It was no use. With an exasperated yell, he felt a sluggishness creep up his legs, resulting in repeated stumbles. Finally, his foot hooked on a root poking up from a field of moss, and he fell forward, planting his face directly into the moss.

It didn't hurt, it actually felt like landing on a soft bed, but Chris struggled to push himself up. His arms refused to hold his weight and crumbled under it. Spitting out bits of moss and a leaf, he growled and tried again. With the same outcome. Like a fish on dry land, he flopped around on the moss, frustrated groans and yells leaving his lips.

Eventually, he stilled. His chest heaved under heavy breaths, there was nothing he could do, but let the fear swallow him whole to take him for a ride. Grunting, he turned onto his back and closed his eyes. Still, the sun shining through the leaves above, let specks of light dance over his lids, turning his field of vision from black, to red, to black again. Tears gathered at the corners of his eyes and ran down his face. An eruption born of the tumult inside of him. Panic, pain, anger, frustration, and sheer terror.

If this was real, then nothing was as he believed it to be. Part of his mind tried to rationalize his situation, even as he lay there, his chest radiating with burning breaths, his heart hammering, and the agony at trying to leave worsening in sync with each of those staccato heartbeats.

It was no use. If any of this had actually been a dream, the searing pain spreading steadily throughout his body, would have surely woken him by now. He needed to get away from the edge, to think clearly, without the pain.

Like a snail, he slowly wormed his way back, still unable to get up and just walk. With a combination of shimmying, crawling and rolling, he made it far enough to sit up.

Gasping for air, he rose to his feet and commanded his shaky legs to get a grip. One step in front of the other. Thankfully – like last time – the pain lessened with each step he took. Exhausted, Chris sank down on the stem of a fallen tree. He bent over and breathed. Sweat pearled down his forehead as he wheezed and rubbed his chest, right where the bullet wound should have been. Bobbing his knees up and down, he relished the absence of pain and even felt the panic ebb from within. As scary as the prospect was, he had to accept facts. He was caught in a strange place – where he magically healed and could apparently feel the heartbeat of trees – and there was no getting out. Not the way he had tried at least. Twice.

As acceptance ran through him, pulling the panic to the side, Chris was left with a bitter taste in his mouth.

With the back of his hand, he wiped his forehead, waiting for the ragged breathing to mellow down.

After a while, he calmed down, only to cringe at his own meltdown. Losing it like that didn't happen to him. He prided himself on keeping a cool head in tense situations. Quick thinking, even in danger. The ability to do that had saved his life a few times already. But he guessed he could give himself half a pass – being rational and weighing facts all his life – who would have guessed shit like this existed? Besides, part of him felt really bad for running, while Emily was emotionally tied like a pretzel. And only this place knew why.

Chris blew out air and dug his naked feet into the moss on the ground. A bitter chuckle left him. Because, sure enough, he felt something tickle his soles. A radiating beat of power. Life.

"That is not unsettling at all," he rumbled, stemming the fear rippling at the edge of his mind. This… new sense was impossible, but clearly there. And it looked like it was getting stronger.

He moved his feet around a bit, deciding to face his discomfort head-on. A myriad of small and big pulses, from varying directions tickled his soles. For long moments he sat there, his eyes closed and his toes curling down then flexing slowly. It was impossible to make out from what the twinges and pulses originated. Where all of it plants and trees? Did he feel animals, too? He had no way of knowing. Probably should ask Em about it.

A twinge, sharper and more prominent than the others hit the outside of his right foot and Chris jerked. "The hell?"

He closed his eyes once more and concentrated. There it was again. It felt like someone flicked a finger against him. Urgent, pinching, again and again. Chris frowned, got up and started walking in the direction of the urgent pinch. What was this new madness? Did it mean something happened? With each step, the urgency built. Had something happened to Em? That thought spurred him on and his heartrate picked up.

He wanted to run toward the urgency, but all he could manage was a pretty fast walk. Otherwise, he lost the feeling.

Ducking under branches, clambering over tree stems and rocks, Chris traversed the forest. If his sense of direction was accurate, he walked away from the cave and rounded the outer edge of the forest, leaving the lake on the right.

The feeling got stronger and now covered both his feet with waves of prickling sensation, allowing him to speed up his steps. Something reddish blinked through the greenery and Chris thought of it being bark, or something similar, but the closer he got, the faster and more intense the waves grew, until they almost hurt.

He stopped short when he saw a doe lying on her side, her belly round and taut as a drum. Her breaths came heavy, loud and almost wheezing. She spotted him, her head lifting off the ground. Those big, bottomless eyes found his, conveying a sense of fear and pain. Something was wrong, and it wasn't him being there.

The doe did not seem to fear him at all, as she lay her head back down and continued breathing in that heavy, wheezing way. Very slowly, Chris crept closer. He had no idea what he would do once he got there, but the waves building and crashing against him couldn't be ignored. She needed help.

Finally, he reached her. Always watched by her, always accompanied by the sound of her heavy breathing. Until it was the only thing he could hear. It was like the forest around them was holding its own breath. No birds chirped and sang, no wind whistled through the trees, and no random call or chirp Chris couldn't place disturbed the silence. Only she.

Heart in his throat, he licked his dry lips.and reached out a hand, still unsure about what to do.

"It's okay. Shh… We'll be fine," the words tumbled from him without thought. His hand met soft fur, and he felt the tautness of her belly beneath. Chris dimly wondered why he wasn't freaking out. He was by no means a nature boy, and had never witnessed anything similar. But strangely, he felt calm and centered. A bit nervous, yes, but not overly so. This was the person he knew kicking back in. The one with the cool head. Relief flooded him at the recognition. "At least, one thing is back to normal," he murmured and stroked over her belly.

This close, with touching her, it was as if he shared part of her discomfort and pain. It vibrated against his hand and traveled up his arm in rippling pinches. Even her fear scampered over his skin and he had to remind himself that none of it was his. It did make it difficult to concentrate though.

He placed his other hand on her too and felt around. "I have no idea what I am doing," he told the doe, who snorted in answer.

"I'll give my best, though." The pain grew the more he moved his hand down and to her back. "Is your little one stuck? Is that the problem?" There was something hard in her belly, directly under her hind leg. "Feels like this shouldn't be here. But how are we going to move it?"

"Feel the lake," Emily's voice said behind him.

Chris jerked his head around to look at her. Her face was red and her chest heaved, looked like she had run from the other side of the lake. Had she felt the same thing and come to help?

"You know what to do, Em. Help her," Chris said, pulling his hands back.

"No. You were called, you must assist." She sank down next to him and placed his hands back on the doe's belly. "You have figured out the problem. The little one's legs are in the wrong position. Feel the lake. Draw from it and help her."

He shook his head, annoyed. "Em, I have no fucking clue what I am doing. Just help her, okay?"

Emily held his hands to the doe's fur with her own. She turned her head and faced him, her beautiful features soft and understanding. "I know you are scared. You feel her. You feel everything. But you can do this. Trust me and do as I say."

For long moments he lost himself in the depth of her gaze. Clear and bottomless. Eyes to drown in. Filled with confidence. In him? Chris swallowed hard against his own nervousness and the doe's fear. "Okay. What do I do?"

"If you have found her, it means you feel the pulses. You have to find the one of the lake. It is slow, steady and deeply powerful. Try it."

"Feel the beat, right." He smiled at his bad joke, but Emily just nodded once.

Chris closed his eyes and felt. Besides the scalding intensity of what the doe radiated, there where thousands of beats and pinches drumming against the skin of his legs where he crouched on the ground. It was impossible.

"Slow. Deep. Powerful," Emily said. "Slow. Deep. Powerful."

The space in which she said the words seemed to slow his frantic heart. Her presence like a soothing balm. Her voice smooth and warming.

Through the countless prickles, hums, and pinches, Chris searched. Some were fast, so fast it was more of a vibration than anything else. Some resembled the sound of knocking, some languidly thumped as if deeply asleep. The longer he spent combing through the sensations, the more of a sense he got for the different kinds. The fast ones could be little animals, the knocking ones weren't as clear, but he was sure that the slow and sleepy ones belonged to the trees.

Digging further he stumbled when a deep, gong-like thrum went through him. "Slow," Emily said.

He sucked in a breath. *Gong*. "Deep." Another breath. *Gong*. "Powerful."

"Found it," he whispered, thoroughly surprised at how he hadn't felt that kind of powerful beat before.

"Follow it, concentrate on it. Only on it." Emily's hands squeezed his encouragingly.

Chris blew out a breath and homed in on the gongs. Soon, everything else fell away. All the pinches and ripples nipping at his legs quieted, and the slow, deep beat filled more of him with each gong. Until he felt like he was vibrating in resonance from head to toe with each beat. Him and... Emily. She echoed the thrum back, a split-second after the lake. Almost as powerful, but even deeper. The power she and the lake sent through him was mind-blowing and nearly made his teeth chatter.

"Got it," he grunted. "Now what?"

"Now you see her. And help."

"What?"

"Open your eyes, Christian."

Slowly he did. Just like he had during the stormy night, when she had shown him the beating of the lake and everything else, he saw the power. The life. It was as if the normal colors around him had turned translucent to a degree, and he could see the life behind it. In shimmering blues, glinting greens, and shiny silver, he saw the beating life. The pure essence of power. The plants around him had tiny flows of it, the trees bigger ones and the doe radiated with small pulses of it. Underneath it all, the ripple of the lake washed through every few seconds. Followed by Emily's own beat. Did she know she did that? Chris wondered.

"Focus on her. See her and help."

Chris looked down to where his hands were and grimaced when he saw through his own fingers and into the very life essence of the doe. He saw the tangled legs of the fawn but had no idea how they should be placed, or how to do it. Just as he was about to ask Emily, shimmering silver enclosed the fawn, then black dripped from the position of its legs, getting more and more. Chris cursed and acted on instinct. He pulled at the steady thrum of the lake and let it fill him up like before. Then he opened himself up, as if he was floodgate, and let the power course through him and to the doe. Two things happened at once.

Pure power washed from his fingertips and into the life-force of the doe and fawn, making them shine and pulse. The blackness got sucked into Chris, who felt it scald up his arms and lodge in his chest.

The fawn's legs untangled and now lay on either side of its head, pointing ahead. He'd done it. With a gasp, Chris sank back, ripping from the doe, Emily and the power. He clutched his chest and let himself fall onto his back. "Fuuuck," he ground out. The world's colors came back, growing solid once more.

"You did it," Emily said, dropping to his side and grinning widely. She hovered over him, giving him a once over, probably to see if he was okay.

As he lay there, Chris swore he had never seen anything more beautiful in his life, and he had just witnessed pure magic. For real. But Emily smiling down at him, with a genuine warmth he had never seen her sport before, was something else. The feeling of the acidic blackness in his chest washed away and he had no idea if it had been on account of the lake, himself, or Emily's smile. He got lost in the soft lines of her face. The delicate curve of her brows, her adorably small nose, the fullness of her lips… their shape. And her eyes. This close, he was able to see that they too resembled what he had seen only moments ago. A swirl of green, blue and silver. Mixed together so subtly that it was only apparent from this close.

Her coppery-red hair blew over his face when a breeze picked up and he swiped at the tickling tresses. With a very slow gesture, he tucked a strand of hair behind her ear. When his index finger grazed the curve of her ear, she shuddered and pulled back. But before she turned from him, Chris saw her eyes widen and the green and blue swirl. What the hell?

Dumbfounded, he sat up, trying to look at her, to see if what he had witnessed had been real. But she was busy getting up. "We should give them space now. She will do the rest on her own," Emily said and reached out a palm to him.

Chris sighed and took it – and was yanked to a stand so quickly his head swam. "Holy shit, woman. What do you eat?"

Emily lifted a brow at him and tilted her head. "Mushrooms, roots, fish, and meat. Sometimes berries. Why?"

Chris had to chuckle at her seriously confused face. "No reason."

She shrugged and backed away from the doe. With little waves, she indicated at him to follow. He glanced at the doe, who watched him with what seemed like gratitude. She still breathed heavy, but she didn't wheeze anymore and the pulse reaching the soles of his feet now were soft and warm. There was still pain, but no more fear.

Unable to process his feelings on the matter, Chris walked from her backwards, keeping his eyes on her as long as possible. Amazing. He had... he had done... Magic?

Chapter Eleven

Christian surprised her. As Emily walked through her forest, followed closely by him, he kept glancing back, a look of utter wonder on his face. He had helped. Instructed by her, but still. The way and speed with which he had followed her words and dove into his abilities was mind-boggling. She had taken longer. But then again, she never had anyone teach her.

A small part of her was sad that he had been called to assist. Normally, these were her responsibilities, but this time, she had clearly felt an intention. The lake had picked Christian. Why? Was it because he was developing and needed to learn? Or was it because of what she had discovered? Was she really someone different than she had thought? Not enough? She swallowed. Human?

Leading them through the forest, she concentrated on the soft grass beneath her naked feet and the small caresses of the leaves hanging low from trees she passed. The forest parted as she led them out, toward the lake, relishing the late mid-day sun on her skin. No matter what, her skin greeted the feeling, her ears the sound of small ripples on stony ground, her tongue the taste coming up from the lake as it grew colder.

"That… that was amazing," Christian huffed out. "I just… dshh." He reached out his hands and made a strange sound. "And the fawn slid into the right position. Oh my, did you know of the sheer power the lake has?" He smiled and slapped a palm to his forehead. "Of course, you do. But, wow! Did you see?"

"I saw. I was there and showed you, remember?"

His hand dropped from his face and he scrutinized her. Emily tried to keep her face straight, but it seemed to not work. It was not as if she had any practice in hiding her feelings from anyone. She stalked ahead and dipped her feet into the lake.

"Are you… jealous?" Chris asked, coming up at her side and leaning over to see her face.

"What? Of course not, do not be stupid." She turned from him.

"You are. I just found her first, means nothing."

"You were called to help. I was not. But that is not the – never mind."

"What's going on, Em?" Chris rounded her.

"Nothing."

"Clearly there is."

She crossed her arms, lifting her head to look at his face. "It does not matter."

Their eyes met and she nearly forgot why she was sad. He was so alien, yet so familiar. Looking at him was both exhilarating and relaxing. Her heart skipped a beat when she thought back to when she had leaned over him. His look back then had been similar to the one she was exposed to now. His green eyes drew her in like the lake did on a full moon. Her bones wanted to sing and she felt like drawing closer to him. Was it because the lake had healed him? Because he was now a part of it?

"Em," he said after a while, seemingly equally enthralled by her as she by him. "It matters."

"It just… took me a lot longer to figure out how to find and work the lake's power. You have done good. Great even. And–"

He reached out and touched her shoulder. His skin on hers zinged through her like static, but Emily didn't feel like jerking away. Rather, she wanted to lean into the touch. *Why?*

"You told me exactly what to do," Christian said. "I would have been useless without you. Thank you for showing me how."

His words made her feel better, in a way her own thoughts had failed to do. She managed a small smile and Chris reacted with his eyes widening a fraction. Had her smile surprised him? That was unusual. At least that was what she thought. Smiles should not surprise, should they? Not knowing frustrated her. As much as her behavior from before still did.

"I should not have snapped at you and run off. I apologize."

Christian took a small step closer. "What happened? Was it the memory, or something else?"

His proximity upped the pull she felt toward him even more. It took a considerable amount of concentration not to reach out herself. Had he been her lake, she would have jumped in. Instead, she focused on his hand on her shoulder, the weight, the subtle prickling scampering over her skin, the goosebumps on her back it inspired. Maybe him being close helped, maybe this… excitement made it easier to talk about it. Whatever it was, Emily was able to cast her memory back, without getting lost in the images and feelings.

"I remembered burning. Dying. I felt my skin burst and crack, felt my flesh melt from my bones. There was darkness after." She bit down on her lower lip, her thoughts – despite his distracting presence – supplied her with enough atrocious details to keep talking till the night came.

"Jeez, Em," Christian rasped, taking a small step closer. "That is horrifying. I can't even imagine going through something like that. No wonder you broke down." He looked thunderstruck.

"How…" she cleared her throat to address her confusion. "How did I forget? I died, Christian. I… I should not have f-forgotten." A chill swept through her, and she shivered despite the afternoon sun.

"Are you cold?" he asked, his expressive face worried.

She shook her head, fighting the chill. "C-can you do what you d-did before? I think it helps."

He looked confused for a moment, then his brows shot up and his lips curved into a smile. His fingers on her shoulder squeezed once and then pulled her against his chest. His arms wound around her, enveloping her in the most curious sense of warmth and safety she had ever felt.

"Better?" he asked.

Emily slowly mirrored him and drew her arms around his middle. Her hands slid up his back where they found the hard softness that was so unique to his body. "Yes. Better," she whispered. If that was true, then why was her heart hammering as if it wanted to leave her chest? More goosebumps covered her, this time, ones of heat and comfort. All of it chased away the painful memories from before and she was able to continue.

"I don't remember why I burned, or anything before it. But what if you are right? What if I was–"

"Human?" Christian suggested.

"Yes. I believed myself to be different from them. I fought them, drove them out. But what if I am exactly the same?" Doubt, heavy and thick, wore her down and she was thankful for him holding her. Even with him against her, she was afraid.

"I am so sorry that happened to you, Em," he rumbled. "But being human isn't so bad. I am one, too. And the lake still chose to heal me. I think it did the same for you."

She shook her head awkwardly against his chest, she refused to pull back from him to do it freely.

"As for the why," his voice hardened, "you screamed something about them coming for you. About them coming for the witch, to burn and drown her."

His words tore at something inside her mind, something closed off. Emily stemmed herself against it. Not now. She was not ready to break apart again. Not so soon. And definitely not in his arms.

"Can we stop talking about it?"

"Of course. But you should know that it will come back. Until you deal with it and face all of it." His hands ran over her shoulder, up the nape of her neck and down again, in soothing strokes.

Emily watched a fish swim closer to them both, investigating. It nipped at her big toe once, then turned and rejoined his school. His smooth movements made small ripples dance up her ankles. She wished she was able to vanish into nothingness, like the fish and his tickling waves. All she could do was hide for a bit longer. "I'm not ready," she conceded.

"You will be," he assured her.

Finally, Emily pulled back a little so she could tilt up her head. "How are you so sure?"

The corners of his lips twitched, but bitterness shone in his eyes. "You survived the memory of burning alive. You can face anything. Besides, we all have to face our own darkness, or it will eventually consume us."

Emily had no idea what he meant with the last sentence, but it seemed to be the root of the bitterness. She would have to ask him about it. Not now, though. Now she needed to explain. "I snapped at you and ran because I was… I did not like needing you to take care of me. I have never needed anyone to help me."

"And I am a human."

"And you are a human. You calmed me and brought me back from horrifying memories. I heard you calling me. It irritated me that you helped without question. This… Needing this, is disconcerting. I do not understand it. Your warmth helps me stem the memories. It is soothing."

His eyes searched her face, and she almost *felt* them roaming, settling first on her eyes then on her lips. Why was her breath shortening? Heat traveled up her neck to nestle on her cheeks and her pulse quickened. "And then there is this," she whispered.

"What?" his hands left her back and cupped her face gently, his thumbs stroking her heated cheeks.

"I… I feel drawn to you. My skin tingles from your touch, my heart races and my breath speeds up. I want something. And I think it is… you? Why? What am I feeling?"

A shuddering breath blew from Christian and he pulled back, letting go of her. "Whoa. I, uhm… I'm sorry." He took a step back, pulling free of her arms. Digging one hand into his hair, he disheveled the brown mess further. "I thought it was… Uhh." He paced a few steps to the left, then turned on his heel and took the same route to the right. The water of the lake, sloshed around his naked feet, making waves splash against her legs. He stopped. "Em…" His hand pulled at his hair again. Those green eyes flitted over her, then to the bank behind her, then to the forest, and back to her. "I'm having a damned hard time controlling myself right now." He released a nervous-sounding laugh and paced again. "I've never… this pull is insane."

That was something she understood. "I know. It is like the pull of my lake on a full moon. When we connect and I am infused with all its power. Whatever this is, it feels similar to that. And I have never been able to resist."

Christian halted, his brows rose and he opened and closed his mouth few times. "I have no idea what half of that was just now, but it sounded way too hot. I'll meet you at the cave, okay? I need a swim. Alone," he added when she happily reached for the hem of her dress.

Disappointed, Emily let her hands sink to her sides.

He stepped up to her, caught one of her hands and placed it on his chest, to feel his racing heart. "I have to leave now, Em. Or I will take us both up on this insane pull. And I am not sure you really want that. Just know I feel exactly the same as you."

He drew back and threw himself into the lake, dressed and all.

With clenching fists, she watched him swim away. It was nearly impossible to not follow. She did not understand. Even the pull toward her lake was different. Just as strong, but in another way. This was… heat and a very strange need. A sensation leaving her tingling from head to toe. Emily decided then and there to follow this feeling. When he was ready.

It looked like they both needed time to adjust to different things. All she knew was that she wanted to be close to him again. To feel his hands on her skin. To get lost in his gaze. To… find out where all of it would lead them.

Her feet crunching on the pebbled ground, she turned from him and walked up the bank. She skipped through the grass and whistled, soon getting answers from various birds. With a smile and feeling tons lighter than before, she made her way up the hill and to the cave. No matter what she would have to deal with, she was glad Christian was there, even if he had just fled.

It was impossible to shake her. Even as he swam far into the lake, only smelling, tasting, and feeling the cool water around him, Chris was unable to drown her out. Her face, the feel of her so close to him… Those words said by her silken voice… He dove under.

The rippling sluggishness of the water didn't help. It neither chased away the image of her, nor his raging hard-on. Chris kicked off the muddy ground, feeling the smooth and slimy algae beneath his feet. His face pierced the water and he spluttered and swam on. With all his might, he tried concentrating on the beauty around him. The golden light reflected by the waves he made, the swishing, gleaming zig-zag of a bunch of dragon flies. Their wings blinked, their shimmering bodies looked like works of metallic green and blue art.

Fish darted around his legs, as if to keep him company, but none of it could hold his attention for very long. Nothing measured up to her. With a heavy sigh, he started swimming in the direction of the bank closest to their hill. By the time he got out of the water, the last rays of sun played with the leaves of trees he passed. Chris shivered from the cold and cursed himself repeatedly for jumping in with all his clothes. The good thing was, it was too cold to sustain any kind of arousal and he smiled bitterly as he trudged up the hill. Served the bastard downstairs right.

Chapter Twelve

When Chris reached the cave, Em sat on a rock outside, overlooking her valley. She looked otherworldly and he nearly paused only to take her in. But he forced himself to continue. Still, he didn't miss the way the wind made her hair dance, and how the last rays of sunlight made her coppery tresses glint, or how her eyes found him and her luscious lips curved into a smile.

"How was your swim?" she asked when he passed her.

"Cold," he murmured.

She frowned and glanced at the cave. "I tried to make fire, but it still scares me a little. And I have no idea how you do it. That magic-flame-thingy of yours surprised me too much."

Chris had to laugh at her pout. "Come on, Em, I'll show you."

She happily slid down the rock, not losing a beat as she landed on rubble and walked over in steady strides.

They entered the cave together and Chris raised a brow when he saw that Emily had rearranged the cave. Their blankets were neatly laid out, his measly belongings sitting neatly on his pallet. Even his shoes were placed next to it. Curious, had he seen how little he owned a week ago, he would have completely lost it. Even now, nervousness fluttered in his belly. Owning nothing meant hunger, it meant being dependent – or getting creative. Chris kept reminding himself how it didn't matter much here. There was nothing threatening him, and no need to fight, lie, steal, or cheat to survive and thrive. But that was just it, the one constant in his life was gone, had been blasted away by a bullet to the chest.

While he pushed at those thoughts and the discomfort they brought, he saw that Emily's pallet was right next to his, putting him between her and the fireplace. This time, a whole other train of thought rushed through him.

Chris picked up his lighter and squatted down, Emily mimicking him with curious eyes. She clasped her knees, the long strands of her hair pooling around her body on the floor. They were impossibly soft, Chris knew that now. As soft as they looked. He turned his head and laughed when he saw what she had done to the fireplace.

Heaps of moss and moldy wood was stacked together in a wet mess.

The outburst of laughter splintered apart the dark thoughts from before, and even tore at the ones regarding Emily. But as she sat next to him, her presence itself like a live flame, limiting the pull toward her wasn't as easy.

"What?" she asked, watching him laugh with drawn brows. They made a straight and angry crease appear between them and she would have looked angry, if there hadn't been so much confusion in her eyes. "Did I do it wrong?"

Chris calmed and picked up a dripping piece of moss. "Sweetheart, nothing this wet will ever burn. Fire needs dry wood to burn."

The crease vanished and she placed a palm on the heap. His breath faltered as the heap started cracking and hissing under her touch. As if she was a sponge, the color of the moss was sucked from it and into her hand. When she pulled back, the heap was dry as bones.

"Like this?" she asked.

He looked from her to the heap and back again. The shadow of a sly smile betrayed her. "You did this on purpose," Chris stated.

Emily shrugged. "Maybe."

"Show off."

She chuckled. "I just wanted to see your face. Worth it." With a little wave, she gestured for him to carry on.

He shook his head and flicked the lighter, then held the flame to the heap. It caught on immediately. Emily shuddered subtly, but otherwise didn't move. Intently, she watched the fire grow, the flames dancing in her eyes. The way she sat there, mesmerized by it, was enthralling to him.

To get his mind straight, he held out his freezing hands and warmed his, by now, numb fingers. It didn't do much good, as soon enough, the wet clothes he wore made him shiver and his teeth chatter. Goosebumps spanned his entire body, adding to the shivers.

"Do you need me to go?" she asked quietly, watching his shaking arms.

Chris stood and turned from her to walk over to his pallet. "No." He drew his clinging shirt over his head and spied a little ledge on the cave wall. Swiftly, he hung his shirt on it and nestled with his pants. Even with his back turned to her, he sensed her looking at him. Or maybe it was just his over-active imagination talking. Yeah, he would go with that. He could deal with leading himself on.

"Do you… uhm… Are you able to leave? This forest, I mean?" he asked, slipping his pants down but keeping his boxers on. He hung his dripping pants next to his shirt and picked up one of the blankets folded neatly on his pallet. With a hiss, he burritoed himself into the blanket and traipsed back to the fire, still covered in goosebumps.

"I cannot," Emily said when he slumped down next to her once more. She flexed and stretched out her toes, inching them closer to the fire bit by bit. "I remember..." the sharp crease between her brows appeared again. "After the burning, I remember coolness. Maybe it was death, but it must have been the lake. I think... I think you are right and it did heal me same as you. Every time I venture to the edge of the lake's influence, my skin burns like crazy."

"Huh." Chris rubbed his hands together and pulled up his knees to rest his chin on them. "You seemed not to feel it when we were there."

"Over time I was able to go a bit further – but only one or two strides more than you. Then I would writhe on the ground, unable to go on." Her gaze turned inward. "The pain is unbearable for long, so I fought my way back each time. Eventually, I never ventured as far." She lay her cheek on her knee, facing him. "I have not been back to the edge for years, before you came."

"Years? You said you have always been here..."

She rolled her eyes. "We both know by now, I have been wrong assuming that. But I have no idea how long it has been, truly. I think I remember back to around eighty summers."

Chris nearly jumped from his skin. "Eighty? You are more than eighty years old?"

"I would assume. Yes. But I have no real way of knowing. I never change. The animals and plants around me die, making way for the next generation, but me? Besides the lake, I am the only constant."

Still reeling with what she had told him, Chris blinked at her. "Y-you look great for over eighty," he stammered, not knowing what else to say.

She smiled. "Right? Although, I cannot compare myself to other women, so I will take your word for it."

A weak laugh wanted to break from his chest but it stopped, resulting in a stricken noise. Chris cleared his throat. "That settles it then. You may have been human once, but clearly are not anymore. My kind does not live as long – especially not looking like…" he waved his arm up and down, indicating at her.

"Does that mean you are now something else, too? More like me and less like them?"

The question hit him square in the chest, unnerving him even more than anything here had before. Fuck all the weirdness, the obvious magic, and the not-being-able-to-leave part. Had the lake turned him into some kind of immortal? "Holy shit," he whispered. Springing to his feet, he rounded the fire in tiny steps, nearly tripping over the blanket multiple times.

He could not leave. And if the lake had done the same thing to him as it'd done to Emily, he wouldn't age. Which meant he was stuck here forever. The panic from earlier threatened to drown him as he paced, cursed, and stumbled through the cave. For a second he felt like laughing, he had prided himself so much on being level-headed for a long time. Since being here he'd been either drowning in panic or slapped with impossibilities. He felt like he was unraveling at the seams.

****

Emily nibbled on her lower lip, anxiously watching Chris pace and ramble. At one point, he almost fell into the fire, and ripped the blanket from his body to free his legs. He dropped it on his pallet and resumed his pacing.

When she wanted to ask if she could help, he held up a hand, cutting her off. It was obvious that her question had just unearthed something serious within him and he needed to work through it. Emily felt a bit bad for being the reason he was upset. But she laced her fingers around her knees and watched him. Waiting for him to either calm or start talking to her again.

Worried as she was, the way the golden light of the flames painted his skin wasn't lost to her. It caressed the muscles of his arms, his back, his stomach and legs. She wondered what his skin would feel like under this kind of light. Was it as warm and soft as it looked? Was his hair? She had noticed that in the sun, strands of his hair looked almost golden. Much the same way the ripples of her lake looked during the last light. Mesmerizing.

When he started pulling at his hair with both fists, Emily stopped her gawking and stood. She stepped into his way when he wanted to walk past her and – while nervousness knotted her stomach – opened her arms to him.

He halted, his expression a mix of frustration and outright fear. His hands sank from his head while he stared at her as though she had just grown a second head. Emily took a step toward him and drew her arms around his middle. She was careful not to squeeze or hold him tightly, because she had no idea if this was what he needed, but he had done the same for her when she had lost it and knew that it felt good being held.

As she gently hugged him, his arms rose and then paused in mid-air. As though he was warring with himself, they started trembling, before he placed his hands on her back and pulled her closer. Emily let out a surprised breath when he dipped his face and buried it in the crook of her neck. His arms around her tightened and she squeezed right back. For long moments, she held him, feeling his frantic breath even out and deepen.

The heat of the fire tickled her legs, but Emily did not worry, all her focus was on him. Her hands skimmed over his back and she was happy to discover his skin was indeed as soft and warm as it looked, even more so. She wanted to snuggle closer and never let go.

"I apologize," he rumbled into her hair, his voice deep and coarse. "Just freaking out a bit at the prospect of… never aging and never being able to leave."

"I understand." Emily squeezed him again, at loss what else she could do for him.

"Thank you. I needed this." He pulled back and she had to lean her head back to look at him. "How did you know?"

She gave him a one-shouldered shrug. "It is what you did for me."

A shaky smile grew on his beautifully curved lips. "I've never had someone do this for me before." His face dipped and he blushed when he looked down his own body. Clearing his throat, he pushed her back further, leaving their embrace. "I uh… I'm sorry about the…"

Emily was a bit disgruntled when he walked to his pallet and twisted the blanket around him once more. "Are you still cold?"

"No. I just don't want to make you uncomfortable."

She tilted her head to the side when he looked at her. "You did not. I liked so much of your skin so close. It feels good touching you. You are as soft as I imagined."

Another one of those stricken sounds left him. "You have to stop saying things like that, Em."

"Why? It is the truth."

"That may be, but you have to understand–"

A flick of power beat against her feet and she went rigid.

"Did you feel that?" Christian asked.

She nodded and jogged to the entrance to look out over the lake and forest. The thrum of power returned, a call from her lake. "I will take a look," she said and dashed out.

"Em, wait!" Christian called after her, but she did not react. Her lake rarely sent out these warnings. It took a lot of energy to reach her on stone. If it deemed whatever was going on important enough, she would heed the warning and investigate.

The sun was down by now, but Emily ran down the hill sure-footed and almost without making a sound. She skidded to a halt once her soles met grass. For a moment she stood and listened. A sharp pinch hit her feet from the right and she launched into a sprint. While she ran, her lake showed her the way through her soles and she followed without missing a beat. The forest around her was too quiet. When she vaulted over a fallen tree, and dashed past the fox burrow, she noticed that no one was out and about to greet the night. No one sang, chirped or croaked. How had she not realized sooner?

For a second, anger at herself lashed through her. She had been distracted. She could not afford being distracted. Her responsibility was to watch and protect.

The pinches got softer and soon tapered out. It meant she was close now. Close to whatever disturbed the forest and had everyone in hiding.

Emily slowed and then crouched down. She was cautious to take deep but quiet breaths and listened past her accelerated heartbeat. Digging for the power of her lake, she pulled at it, opening herself up to receive the means to fight anyone or anything coming her way.

Something rustled to her right and footfalls sounded through the dark. A twig broke underneath a shoe.

She hid behind the stem of a tree and spied around it. Two people came into view. The silver of the waning moon painted them with cool light as they broke from the brush and stomped into the meadow splayed before her. Both carried the same bended sticks that made such awful noise and had nearly killed Christian.

She bared her teeth and felt the power flow through her. Like sluggish ripples of water, it coated her from head to toe, filling her up and making her body vibrate with strength.

Just as she was about to fling the power at them, a hand closed around her mouth from behind. A strong arm circled her arms, pressing them against her sides and then she was yanked back behind the tree. Her first instinct was to let the power blast from her, taking the attacker with it and blowing him to pieces, but when she sucked in a breath, she smelled him. Christian had followed her.

He twisted her in his grasp, so they were face to face. Holding one finger to his lips in a shushing gesture, he let go of her. "They have guns," he breathed.

Emily raised a brow at him. "They are in my forest. They need to leave."

"Agreed. But let's see what they are up to first."

She glared at him for a moment.

"Please, Em. They could just be lost."

With a curt nod, she turned from him and leaned past the tree. The men had cleared the meadow and headed for the lake directly now. Silent as the night, Emily followed. Christian's steps behind her were loud to her ears, and she had to slow more than once for them to stay undetected. How in the name of the lake he had been able to sneak up on her just then was a mystery.

Once she heard the crunch of their boots on the pebbled bank, she snatched Christian's hand and pulled him behind one of the trees lining the lake.

Mist crawled over the lake, masking the shimmering ripples and lending an eerie feel to the scene. The men stood on the bank, their dark silhouettes clear against the pale, moonlit bank. They spoke in hushed tones, but as everything and everyone was so quiet, their words echoed over the lake.

"You sure it was here?" one asked, looking around. His voice was jittery and nervous, much like a small bird.

"Positive," the other one said, then kicked a pebble into the lake. Emily bristled at the feel of the stone hitting the water. Deeply tapped into the power as she was, she felt every minute disturbance of the water.

"There is nothing here," the nervous man stated.

"I can see that, you numbskull," the other answered. "But you saw her, and what she did. I'm telling you, we find her, and take her. She – or whatever she is able to do – will be worth a lot to someone."

A grunt sounded from her side and Christian's hand squashed hers. She looked at his face and froze. It was pulled into an angry mask, frightening her. Emily had not known he could look this dangerous. The intensity shining from his eyes was chilling as he pulled free of her and seemed to want to leave the treeline.

Emily remembered the bang, and him in the water, bleeding. She reached out and pulled him back. There was no way she was about to let him get hurt again.

He tore at her hold, but she easily drew him back. She had just pulled him behind one of the trees when the men turned in their direction.

"Did you hear something?" the nervous one asked, pointing his stick, or "gun," as Christian called it, around.

"Don't shit your pants, Clarence," the other one said. "We're in a forest, there are bound to be animals around."

While Emily pressed Christian with his back to the tree, holding him in place with a hand to his sternum, wrapping him in the power, she glanced at the men.

"Yeah, you're probably right. It's awfully quiet though," Clarence said.

"Let. Me. Go," Christian whispered.

"So, you can get hurt by those sticks again? I think not." Emily stared him down, until he relaxed somewhat. She reigned in the power, seeing him come to his senses as he nodded at her once. Wary of his still dangerously angry face, she made sure to keep him in place.

"What now?" Clarence asked.

"We scout some more, then report back, Gus will want an update. As soon as he has healed fully, we'll come back with backup and get her."

A chill forked down her spine, tingling with dread. They were talking about her, and the man who had hurt Chris, the one she had thrown around. These two were part of the group who had hunted Chris. They would be back? For her and her power?

Another glance told her that the men continued on along the bank, their steps crunching on the ground as they went. She should kill them where they stood. Rip them apart and dump their remains outside of the border. As a warning. Just as she made the decision to follow, Christian raised a hand, cupping hers to his chest. "If I can't go, neither will you."

The anger burning in his eyes was mirrored in her chest, but she could not hold him in place and annihilate the intruders at once. And she was not about to let him get hurt on her behalf, even if he seemed more than ready to let loose. A shaky breath danced from her lips. The danger radiating from him was alien. It did not fit with the man she had come to know.

An ear shattering bang had them both jumping. Emily raced from the treeline in time to see a four-legged body rush back into the forest.

"Holy fuck!" Clarence screamed. "What is that?"

"You bloody moron," the other man yelled. "That was just a doe. Stop shooting at everything that moves. She'll have heard that. We have to beat feet."

Her eyes fell on the two men and acidic wrath flared to life inside her. Grabbing hold of the power, she ran for them. She heard Christian's loud steps behind her, but knew she would easily outrun him. By the time he would catch up, there was not going to be much left of the two men. They spotted her in that moment and started sprinting down the bank as though the hounds of hell were nipping at their heels. They would not be fast enough.

With an outraged cry breaching her lips, she clawed at the power and willed her legs to move faster. Then she felt it. A bitter taste entered her mouth as pain sliced into her feet from the direction the doe had fled to. They had hit her. Hurt her. Gnashing her teeth, Emily veered off to the left, following the pain.

Chapter Thirteen

Chris felt his pulse beating behind his ears, as rage pummeled through his insides like a rabid beast. But when he tried to keep up with Emily, stark fear entered the equation. If she reached them, they were bound to shoot her, too. His eyes widened when she picked up speed, barreling down the bank faster than was humanly possible.

He tried to run faster, but there was no way he'd be able to intervene in any way. In that moment, pain thrummed through him, it was a flutter he knew, because he had felt her earlier. The doe.

Apparently, Emily had felt the same, because she turned from her hunt and raced straight into the forest. Chris shot one last look at the men, who ran for their lives, then followed her.

They didn't have to go far. The doe hid in a bush, droplets of blood leading up to it. Emily slowed to a walk and softly spoke to her.

"They hurt you. I am so sorry. Come, love, let me take a look at that."

The doe hobbled to face her, but she did not come out of the bush. Her breaths had gone heavy, reminding Chris of earlier during the day.

"Can we do anything to help her?" he asked when he reached Emily.

The doe's ears twitched and she sniffed, her huge eyes switching from Emily to him.

"We can, but it seems like you have to lure her out," Emily said. "She recognizes your voice."

"My voice?"

"She knows you helped her before. She trusts you."

"You want me to… ask her to come out?"

"Yes." Emily placed one hand on her hip and glanced at him. "Is that very hard to understand?"

"Uh, no. Nope. It's just… Never mind. I'll give it a try." He cleared his throat and reached out a hand to the doe. "Uhm. Will you come out of there, sweetie? We can help you, but you need to trust us." He felt slightly stupid as he tried to convince a wild animal to leave her hiding place. Especially with Emily next to him. "I promise you'll be safe."

The doe took a tentative step forward, her large eyes not leaving him.

"That's it, sweet thing. You can trust us." Trying hard to keep his voice level, Chris beckoned her closer. With tiny steps, each one pulsing with pain, she emerged from her hiding place.

"Very good. We'll meet halfway, okay?" He slowly walked up to her and held out his hand.

The doe sniffed his palm, her wet nose bumping against his fingers softly, then she took another step and let him run his palm up her face.

Emily followed and let her hand be sniffed, too. "Good job. You have a very natural and genuine way with her, you know?" She took the doe's head into both hands. "What were you doing at the lake, love? You knew there was danger."

The doe snorted and looked past them, toward the lake.

"Your babe? It is somewhere near the lake?" Emily asked.

Another snort answered her.

"Right. We will get you there." She followed the river of blood flowing from the doe's left shoulder with steady fingers. "This has to come out, then I can heal you." Emily looked at Chris. "Will you step back a bit, please?"

Having no idea what she was about to do, Chris did as she asked. He cursed when Emily carefully wrapped her arms under the doe's belly and simply picked her up. As if she was carrying a puppy, Emily made her way back to the lake. The doe didn't move, seemingly knowing she was receiving help.

Chris quickly followed, dumbstruck by what he was witnessing. He guessed he would have been able to carry the doe, with a little effort. But Emily? The picture before him made no sense to his brain.

"Need help?" he asked.

"Oh no, thank you. She is quite light."

"Seriously?"

Emily gave him a quick smile then saw that the doe's head swiveled to the right. "You can look for her fawn in that direction and make sure it is okay."

Chris paused to watch Emily continue down to the bank. He shook his head and walked to the right. It wasn't easy seeing anything in the dark, so he tried to concentrate on the thousands of beats tickling his feet. It also wasn't easy, as he had to ignore the doe's pain to do so. He took a few calming breaths and closed his eyes. As he felt deeper, he soon noticed an array of tiny and big beings around him. A small heart fluttered with fear. It was very close. Chris opened his eyes and followed the feeling. In a nest of higher grass, the fawn lay on its side, making itself as small as possible.

"Hey there," Chris greeted the fawn. "We have met before. Not that you'll remember me, but I was kind of your… midwife? Oh my god, this is weird. Uhm…" He sank down on his hunches and was rewarded with the fawn lifting its head. He held out his hand and it sniffed.

"There you go, all reacquainted. You up for coming with me? I'll take you to your mom."

The fawn blinked at him, its velvety eyes deep as wells. It stayed put.

"I guess you're well-hidden here. I'll go and make sure you mum will find you once Emily is done helping her, okay?"

The fawn sniffed again, then got up. Its sticklike legs traipsed through the grass, and its fluffy little tail wagged once.

"Coming with me?" Chris asked and got up when the fawn approached him. He took a few steps back and the little guy followed.

"Looks like you are. Good, let's go see mum."

The lake wasn't far and soon enough, Chris had coaxed the fawn from the treeline and to the bank.

Once they reached it, Chris saw Emily and the doe standing in the water, mist billowing around them. Emily had – of course – taken off her dress and scooped water from the lake onto the doe's shoulder with both hands. Then she placed her palms on the wound and closed her eyes. The doe jerked once but didn't run off.

As Chris marveled at the scene before him, the fawn started bleating loudly at his side and the doe gave a soothing grunt, but still didn't move.

"All is well now," Emily said and gently pushed at the doe. She stalked from the lake and bent down to her fawn. Their noses touched before the doe lifted her head and nudged Chris in the chest once. He stroked her neck, eliciting another nudge. Her bottomless eyes seemed to look straight into his soul. A cloud of gratitude swallowed him, then she walked around him, the fawn prancing away next to her.

Chris saw them both vanish in the forest, sighing with relief. The sound of sloshing water behind him made him face Emily as she emerged from the lake. Her skin was glistening in the moonlight and mist parted around her as she drew closer. She looked otherworldly. Spellbound, he held his breath until she reached him.

"You should have let me kill them," she stated, her eyes swirling with shimmering green and luminous blue. That dark and dangerous power, sucking the light away, chilling him. But unlike the first time he had sensed it, it didn't scare him.

"Likewise. They were here searching for you. And they will be back."

Emily rested her fists on her hips. "Yes. Which is why I should have killed them."

"They would have hurt you."

"It does not matter."

"Jeez, Em, of course it fucking matters."

Her angry eyes met his. "You still do not understand. My responsibility is to protect this place and tonight I failed. I should have been vigilant. I should have felt them the moment they entered the forest. Because I did not, she got hurt." She pointed at the forest, then shook her head. "I was too distracted by you to notice. It cannot happen again."

"Are you saying this is my fault?"

"No. The fault lies with me." The sense of danger lifted from her and her shoulders slumped. "You cannot leave, yet you are the root of my distraction. I do not understand it, but since you got here, you triggered memories I had buried. You bring me joy and frustration. My waking thoughts are bound to you and I cannot shake them." She paused, then pivoted toward her lake. "I wish you could leave, for both our sakes. At least the loneliness from before was known."

Her words triggered many things. Anger, heat, annoyance, sadness. Chris breathed out and concentrated on her beat. The sadness he heard in her voice was prominent in her energy, as was guilt and an unfathomable amount of rage.

"The cave will be yours. You should stay there and not look for me. If they come back, do not engage. I will deal with them." Emily bent down, scooped up her dress and pulled it over her head.

"No."

She faced him with a raised brow. "No?"

"No. I led them here, I will deal with them."

"Christian, you cannot. You have but experienced a lick of the full power the lake can bestow. You do not know enough to use it in a fight."

He took a step closer to her. "So, teach me, like you did today. Show me how to use the power. Then we can both keep this place safe."

A smidge of doubt flashed across her face. He didn't know why, but the doubt seared right into his chest. "You don't think I can learn?"

"On the contrary, I believe you will excel at everything I could show you."

"Then what? It is a good idea, Em. You don't have to do everything alone."

Her wary gaze met his. "I am unsure that teaching you will result in a good outcome."

"What?"

"You are still very much one of them, what if you use what you learned to do harm?"

A lone, disbelieving laugh left his lips. "I should fucking hope so. We are trying to protect this place after all."

She didn't answer, just looked at him. And he understood. "Y-you think I would hurt you?"

"I have no way of knowing."

Chris spluttered, searching for words befitting his outrage.

"I need to think," Emily said. "Please wait by the cave. I will search the forest and see if I have overlooked anything else." With that, she jogged away from him, following the deep footprints Gus' men had left behind as they fled.

"Em. Emily! What the hell?" She was gone within seconds, leaving him standing on a moonlit bank of pebbles, the mist from the lake wafted around him. As the night sounds picked up, signaling safety, Chris stood at a loss for words. Hurt that she would think so little of him.

Chapter Fourteen

Emily was thorough. She searched the forest, from surrounding the hill with the cave, to the tall oak marking the border, past countless animals and old tree-friends. All was back to normal. The intruders had mowed a path of destruction on their way out, but they had not hurt another being.

The connections she felt pulsed normally. It was the steady chase, catch and furrow of the night. The languid pulse of the trees spoke of normality and growth. An owl hooted, before gliding from a branch, diving down to snatch up an imprudent mouse. Frogs croaked their night song and crickets chirped from the tall grass.

Emily walked carefully, feeling each step fully, listening for danger, and scanning her surroundings. Chris was right, if they worked together, they could protect this place better. And he had led the other humans here in the first place. Still… the danger she had felt around him when he had gotten angry… She was unsure if she could face it if directed at her. He learned too fast, and it scared her.

Emily reached the lake and waded into the water. She picked up the hem of her dress and balanced on one foot, while pulling the other through the sluggish water, creating ripples.

"Why?" she asked softly. "Why have you healed him? Is it because you trust him? Is it because you know the depth of my loneliness?" As always, her lake did not answer. Its beating heart gave her comfort, though. Slow. Deep. Powerful.

"It has always been only us. And I could really use a little direction here. Do I trust him fully? Without knowing that much about him?"

Silence. Emily sighed, knowing the decision was hers alone to make.

While she waded through the water, until she was close to the hill, she thought on it. He had come to the doe's aid, without knowing what to do, but fully intending to help. He had a gentle and natural way with all living this, even with her. He understood her fears, helped her voice them and held her when they got too much. But that unbridled wrath… And he had told her his usual nature was to trick people. Was he doing the same with her?

She ascended the hill and soon stood before the entrance of their cave. Something shifted inside her when she saw the golden flicker of fire dance against the limestone walls. More than any other place – apart from the lake – this piece of the forest felt like home. Because of him.

Emily took a bracing breath and walked up the last few steps. Chris sat with his back to the entrance, wearing only his pants. Just like had while following her a while back. They still had to be wet from his swim. A small smile appeared on her lips when she thought about his strange of obsession with being dressed. It was bizarre.

"Decided to talk to me again, have you?" his voice rumbled. Emily frowned. It sounded angry. She shook off the feeling and walked past him. The fire warmed her, but discomfort still accompanied the warmth as she sat down a little further from it.

"I have searched the whole forest. We are alone once more."

Chris' green eyes found hers and she was taken aback at his expression. There was hurt, and anger. Not the dangerous kind she was afraid of, but it startled her, nonetheless.

"Great, Em. Terrific, even. So, what are you doing back here?" His tone was harsh, different from anything she was used to.

"What… I do not understand."

"Weird. Me neither. If I am so dangerous and untrustworthy, why even come back here at all? I could turn on you any minute." He gave her a hard glare, then picked at a piece of lint on his hopelessly dirty pants.

"I only told you what I felt. I do not know you and I am–"

"Sorry, but that is just bullshit. You know me better than anyone in this world. You can feel me, just like I feel you. Tell me, Em, what exactly is your problem with me? Cause you seem drawn to me, but you are afraid?" He spread out his hands in front of him. "I don't get it."

She held his disbelieving and frustrated gaze for a few moments before pulling up her knees and studying how her nails shimmered softly in the firelight. "You told me your way of living was not… decent. That you lived by tricking people. And when we were down there, and I stopped you from going at the two men…" Emily looked at him and worried her lower lip. "Your anger. It was dark. I felt waves of danger radiate from you and I felt like… It does not fit who I have come to know."

He blinked, confusion entering his features. "You mean you could feel it as dangerous?"

She nodded.

"Was it like a pressure, pushing at you?"

Emily tilted her head a bit. "Yes, it was."

"And the light seemed to be sucked away around me?"

"Yes… How do you–"

"You do the exact same. When you draw on the power of the lake while angry."

"I-what?"

"When you told me to leave on the first day, while we ate mushrooms. You told me to leave because I made fun of you. It was the same. A dark pressure, followed by the light being sucked away around you. Freaked me out to no end."

"I… I apologize. Now it makes sense that I did not recognize you, it scared me."

A huff sounded from him. "Yeah, it can definitely be freaky. I didn't know it happened to me, too."

"Looks like you unconsciously drew on the power."

Chris grabbed a piece of wood from a stack and put it on the fire. Emily noticed how he was careful about it, letting as little sparks erupt as possible and her heart warmed toward him. He did it for her benefit, because he knew she was afraid of it. This was him. The man she was getting to know. Someone who cared. She had been wrong about him from the very beginning.

"Well, they were talking about coming for you, capturing you like some fucking prize." A scowl bled onto his handsome features and that same darkness flickered around him. Now Emily saw it for what it was – energy drawn from the connection.

"I will teach you. If you are still interested."

The darkness vanished instantly and his gaze snapped to hers. "I am. I want to protect this place."

****

Chris stopped himself from adding, *And I need to protect you.* Because it was what he felt, what had gone

128

through him earlier at the riverbank. The rage engulfing him if he even thought about Gus' men was monumental. He didn't know if his feelings drew on the lake, or if the lake infused him with the wrath, but when he pondered it for a moment, he remembered coming back up here. Pissed off as he had been, he still worried about her. He wanted to be at her side, looking for danger, eradicate it, knowing her to be protected.

She had not needed him. And she probably still didn't. But he would help where he could. It was his fault she was now on Gus' hit list, after all. And he understood her hesitation. When he had first sensed the darkness of her anger, he had fled. It was only fair to be thrown off by something that crass.

"Then it is settled. We will start tomorrow." Emily pulled her dress down over her knees, so she looked like she was sitting in a tent. Her toes dug into the sand and flipped up a tiny rock, sending it flying into the fire. "I will stay awake, you can sleep."

"Not a chance, sweetheart. We take turns."

When her disgruntled face made the sharp crease appear between her brows he chuckled. "You aren't alone in this anymore, remember?"

****

"This is impossible, Em," Chris grunted.

"It most definitely is not. Concentrate. Feel the beat all around you, use it."

Chris and Emily stood in the lake up to their hips. The morning sun heated his exposed skin and birds sang from nearby trees, prompting Emily to hum along from time to time. She had woken him close to dawn, rolling herself up on the pallet next to him to sleep a few hours.

He had watched her sleep, relishing her trusting to watch over her for a while. Chris supposed even relinquishing that short time to him was a step in the right direction. He did hope she would let him help more in the future. But he understood it was a journey for her.

She had stirred when the sun came up and stated that he would be responsible for breakfast, which was how they'd ended up in the lake.

Emily told him to call on the fish. Their energy was slippery though, and every time he thought he got one to come closer, it slipped from his mental grasp. It didn't help his concentration that the ripples around them nipped and kissed Emily's toned stomach, or that her perfect breasts swayed softly whenever she moved.

She crossed her arms. "Close your eyes. Feel them."

Chris did as she said, skimming his palms over the water at his sides.

"Their energy is smooth, drifting. Like smoke, or mist. It slips easily."

Chris snorted. "I have noticed."

"What would you do to draw on such an energy?"

"Dunno. Thoughts?"

One of her silvery laughs echoed across the lake. "Neat try, scoundrel. Now, call on them."

Chris breathed past his chuckle and concentrated. Closing his eyes was definitely working. But the sheer abundance of life around him was distracting, and the lake itself was thrumming with those deep pulses every few seconds, overshadowing all else.

Jitters of small beings vibrated against his submerged skin and it was hard singling one out. He followed a few, but they slipped away effortlessly. It was like chasing flies that seemed to sense when one got too close, then buzzed off.

Chris did not give up, but time went by and when he opened his eyes again, increasingly frustrated, the sun was already high in the sky.

"I'm not getting this," he admitted, wiping his lids with wet fingers.

"Catching fish is the hardest part. Due to their evasive nature."

"Great, give me the most difficult lesson first, why don't you?"

"Are you giving up?" Her eyes glittered with mirth.

"Never." Chris shut his lids firmly and tried again. A flutter of slippery energy zipped past him and he reached out. It was like stretching a muscle he had never used, and when he felt a connection forming to the flutter, he tugged at it, overly excited. The connection evaporated like smoke in the wind and he let out a frustrated grunt.

Waves hit his belly as Emily moved through the water. She came up behind him, reached around and took both his hands in hers. What felt like sparks of electricity prickled over his back when her torso bumped against him softly. A hiss left his lips and he cleared his throat.

"Steady. Slow. You have to pull continuously, or they slip away," Emily rumbled behind him. Her breath fanned over his shoulder and goosebumps rose as a result. Chris had the dim notion that whatever she would do next wouldn't register in his mind. Her hands clasping his, the warmth of her almost touching his back, and her tickling breath distracted him too badly. All he had wanted to do was turn around, sink his lips to hers and hold her close.

While Chris was busy pushing at the thought of how her lips would taste, and how her naked body would feel, sliding against his, she drew his hands over the water in languid circles. *Did she understand what she was doing to him?*

Her chest met his back solidly, and his breath hitched. Emily inched closer, pressing herself to him, and he could feel her heartbeat racing. It was maddening. He bit down on the inside of his cheeks to stop himself from turning in her hold.

"There. Feel that?" she whispered, her words drifting over his shoulders in tickling waves.

"Uh hu?" was all he managed to get out. He had no idea what she was talking about.

"It is close, big. Old. His energy is steadier." Emily skimmed his hand to the right, directing him. Then he felt it. Through the hustle and bustle of the smaller fish, there was something else.

"You can connect," she said. "Gently."

Tentatively, Chris reached out and felt the connection forming.

"Good. Now invite him over. Open yourself to him."

Slippery cold washed into the connection and Chris' first instinct was to tug, but Emily squeezed his hand. "Steady. Do not jerk or tug. Just draw him to you."

As if he was taking a deep breath, Chris tried to manifest what she told him. Lo and behold, the connection strengthened and the fish floated their way. When his sleek body glided under Chris' palm, he almost jumped in surprise, but Emily held him still. The slippery cold was filled with age, heavy with a full life and the knowledge of having fathered generations of offspring. It was amazing.

"Good job," she murmured. "Now let go."

Releasing a breath, Chris let the connection fizzle away. The energy of the fish was still there, slipping and sliding against his own, but it was separate now.

Emily circled her arms around him, still holding his hands as she hugged him to her. "That was great. Well done."

He could be mistaken, but it seemed like her voice was a tad deeper than before. And as before, her heart still hammered against his back, indicating… something.

Too soon, she let go of him and rounded him, bringing distance between them. His back felt cold, but Chris told himself to get a grip, or he would learn nothing at all.

Emily sank down until the water sloshed over her shoulder and only her neck and head poked from the surface. Her long hair fanned out in dark, wet strands and she giggled when the fish swam into her outstretched hands. She stroked him and smiled.

"You still have much to do, young one. Go." She pushed him away, but left her arms outstretched and closed her eyes. As Emily stilled completely, her face drawn in concentration, Chris didn't dare to move. All he could do was watch.

The sunlight danced on the surface, making drops of water sparkle on her neck and face. Dragonflies zapped past them and the water rippled. The ripples grew and buzzed, energy pulsed around them as a swarm of fish surrounded them both.

One broke formation and slunk into Emily's hands. "You honor me, old friend," she told him. Straightening, she pulled the fish from the water and kissed his scaly side. Chris' jaw dropped when he felt the steady energy of the fish being surrendered to Emily. A second later, none was left and the fish stilled in her hands.

"Did you just kill it?" Chris asked.

"No. He gave his life willingly. To sustain us. Just like the plants, roots, and mushrooms I eat, I ask first. I protect them all, so they all keep me fed in turn."

He gawked as she waded away, toward the bank. He had never thought about the circle of life like that, but it made resounding sense to him. And her guilt-ridden face from the night before came to mind. She truly felt like she had failed her precious forest. Failed in protecting all its inhabitants.

With a new sense of purpose, he followed her from the water.

Chapter Fifteen

Emily had been right, drawing in fish was the hardest part. As she taught him how to read the different pulses, how to listen and decipher what many of them meant and to whom they belonged, Chris felt his understanding of it all grow exponentially. She told him it was important to understand the small things before she would introduce him to the full force of the lake. It made sense, but as the days wore on, tension hovered around them like a cloud.

"I have to learn more, Em. Faster." Chris followed the direction of a dull, fuzzy pulse to a mound of mushrooms. "And you have to sleep more." He knelt at the trunk of a tree and threaded his fingers through bits of grass, swiping it to the side to reveal a cluster of mushrooms.

"You are going as fast as you can. Using your power can drain you." She crouched at his side and cut off a couple of caps, then patted the rest and blanketed it once more with grass.

"What do you mean?"

Emily tucked the mushrooms into a bag Chris had made for her. During one night when she had slept, he had ventured to the old houses, found the chest in the only one still standing and rummaged through it. Returning with a patch of leather, he had worked on the pouch for the remainder of the night. He smiled as he thought back on how her eyes had swirled and lit up with joy when he had presented her with it.

Since then, she carried it wherever she went.

"The lake gets its power during the special night. When the moon is full. I – or I guess this time we – will be drawn to it by a force stronger than you can imagine. Once inside, the entire lake will be suffused with colors, then it happens."

"What happens?"

"Everything is replenished. All the lake and I used over the course of the month will be filled up."

"You worry we used too much? Is the energy limited?"

She gave him a half shrug and strutted on, expecting him to catch up. "I have no idea. I have never used this much myself, but I can feel my strength waning. It worries me, yes." When he reached her side and they traversed the forest together, she threw him a little smile. "But you have to learn, so we can defend what is ours."

"Emily. You have to sleep more. You barely let me take watch and you spend your days drawing on your power to help me along. You need a break."

She took his hand and laced their fingers, something she had taken to doing when leading him places. Every time she did, a jolt of heat shot through him and Chris wondered how much longer he would be able to resist pulling her to him and follow the insane pull toward her. At least, it wasn't only him fighting it. He felt her heated gaze on his skin whenever he turned away. She found excuses to touch him, snuggled up to him when she let herself sleep, and she frequently helped him practice calling on fish. With her naked chest against his back. Chris knew it was the main reason he was still unable to catch one on his own, but he enjoyed it too much to tell her.

****

Emily felt the warmth of his fingers in hers. She reveled in the prickling sparks of heat, traveling from their touch and up her arm.

She did need a break, but the dread hanging over her concerning the men coming back, rendered her unable to. Even when she did sleep, it was never long enough and she woke often from dreadful nightmares. Something she had not told him was how her dreams brought her closer to the memories she had buried each night. Maybe it was the anxiousness she felt overall, drawing them out, but whatever it was, they loomed at the back of her mind. As much as she needed rest, she also needed the past to vanish from her mind.

"I will sleep once they have come and we chased them away forever."

"That might be too late, Em," Chris mused. "What if you have completely worn yourself out and they arrive?"

She pressed her lips together. "Not likely."

"Dammit, Em. You aren't made of steel. You have limits. Let me take a whole night's watch, just once."

"Maybe tomorrow."

Chris pulled his hand from hers. "You are stubborn as an old mule. It's exhausting."

Emily clasped nothingness between her fingers, feeling the loss of his touch. "You caring so much is sweet, but I do not need it."

He threw his arms in the air, exasperated. "Of course, you fucking don't. I am Emily, The Lady of the Lake, I need nothing and no one," he said in a laughable imitation of her voice.

"You are being childish."

"So are you!" His angry stare found her and she glared right back. "I'm a grown-ass man, I can take on more to relieve you a bit. You just have to let me."

She did not answer, partly because she was afraid to tell him about her nightmares, and partly because he angered her to the point of snapping at him.

"You know what? I am off to the lake for a swim and to practice. Alone. You can find me when you are ready to talk." Chris huffed and stomped off, finding the direction toward the lake with ease.

She snorted as she watched him storm away, pivoting and delving deeper into the forest. When she came up to the tall oak, marking the border, she paced a bit back and forth, blind to the softness of moss beneath her feet, and deaf to the song of birds and the rustle of the wind. Worn out by her constant need to be vigilant, her lack of sleep, and hurt by the fight she and Chris just had, she sank down between the trunks of a tree opposing the oak. He was right, her exhaustion went deep, and she was doing no one a favor by driving herself onward. But she had no choice. Did she?

As Emily leaned her back against the tree, she tilted her head up, feeling specs of sun dance over her face, filtered by the thick canopy above her. The steady and firm pulse from the tree in her back calmed her a bit. Stretching out her legs, she wiggled them around, picked a bug from where it was busy scampering up her knee and sat it down on a root protruding from the ground at her side.

If only the nightmares let her sleep longer than a few minutes at a time. If only she could get past the ever-nudging memories at the back of her – Emily straightened. Maybe there was a way she could silence them.

****

"Chris. Christian?" Her voice floated up to him, small and… anxious? Chris bobbed around on one toe, having ventured deep into the lake, to where he almost couldn't stand.

Emily waved from the bank, beckoning him over. Dread slid over him. Had they come?

He dove under and pushed himself off the ground, piercing the veil of water with his head a moment later. Quick as he was able, he swam to shore.

"What's going on?" he asked when he was able to wade from the lake.

She knotted her hands together, looking nervous. "I need your help. If you were serious about offering it."

Struggling to catch up with the whiplash she was putting him through, he nodded. "I was. What do you need?"

"I am ready, Chris. Ready to face the houses, and my memories. But I need your help doing so."

"Now? Em, I don't think–"

"*You* said I had to face my fears, in order to overcome them, or they would eat me alive. I am ready to do so."

Chris gave her a once over. "You sure?"

"I am." Her knuckles whitened from how hard she was knotting her fingers, her swirling irises looking chaotic and wild. "Let's go." She reached out, grabbed his hand and pulled him with her. Walking around the lake at a brisk pace, they soon came upon the destroyed village. The closer they got, however, the slower Emily's steps became. Her hand trembled in his, and while she nibbled at her bottom lip and tucked her hair back behind her ear with her free hand repeatedly, her wild eyes hadn't calmed.

"We can turn back, if you want."

"No. I am ready," she huffed out. "I am ready." That last sentence was barely more than a whisper and seemed to be more for her own confidence than to reassure him.

When they walked from the trees and stood in front of the burned and crumbling houses, Emily's breath had accelerated to the point of sounding like she was hyperventilating.

"Em, you can't force these things. I don't think this is the right time."

"You said I had to face it. Now help me and let me do what I need to."

Chris heaved out a sigh and shook his head. "No, Em. I will not. This will not help you."

She twisted to face him. "What do you mean?"

"Look at you. You are shaking just standing here. You're completely out of it. I can't help you like this."

"You mean you will not?" Disappointment entered her expressive face.

"Not like this. But I have another idea. Follow me."

Emily glanced from him to the houses and back to him. She nibbled her lower lip. Nestled with a strand of hair.

"Trust me." Chris squeezed her hand once.

"I do."

He smirked at her and tugged on her hand until she followed him. Leading her away from the ruined village and to a small meadow surrounded by trees on one side and with a clear view of the lake on the other, he sat down. Already her nervous hair tugging subsided and her breathing calmed a bit.

"I know it's the place back there that scares you, and if you go through your memories there, it will make it harder, you'll be unable to control what hits you. Here, we are safe, right?"

She pulled at blades of grass without ripping them, just gentle tugs. "I think so."

"Okay. Now, close your eyes."

Her wild eyes met his and she blinked a few times, then closed her lids and shimmied a little to sit more comfortably.

"You remember that night."

A small nod.

"You remember what the people screamed at you."

Her lip trembled. "To kill the witch."

"Did you know any of them?"

Both her brows drew together. "I knew every single one."

He felt like cursing as a surge of anger bubbled to life inside his gut. "Who are they? Picture one and tell me about them."

Her frown deepened and she opened and closed her mouth a few times. "I remember Beth, Elizabeth. She was a... friend. She... screamed for them to kill me. I-I knew her since we were little. Why would she...?" A hiccup raked her and tears dropped from her long, dark lashes.

Wanting nothing more than to stop, Chris forced himself to go on. "What happened, Emily?"

"I-I... it is hazy. I do not want to..." A sob tumbled from her and she went rigid. "Oh no."

Quick as he could, he scooted over, placed his legs on either side of her and gently pulled her back to rest against his chest. She grabbed his hands and pulled them around her shivering form.

"I'm right here, Em. You can remember. You are safe," even as he said it, his voice cracked. Looking and feeling her unravel as she let go and dove into her past was beyond any pain he had ever experienced. Nothing came close to seeing her inner torture. He had faced all his demons alone, but he would make damned sure she did not.

As he hugged her tightly, rocking them both from side to side, she sobbed. "I saved him. And they said it was witchcraft. I managed to convince them of the healing herbs I used, but then… Lukas… he…" Tears fell from her face and landed on his arms.

"I got you, Em. Open your eyes whenever you want to stop. You can break free at any time."

Pressing her back closer to him, she let him know she understood. Then she wailed, and screamed.

Chapter Sixteen

The houses looked different in her memory. Mostly built with plywood, supporting reed-rooves. Only Beth's was built of stone, as she was the mayor's daughter. Beth, who loved gossip and had adorable black curls. Her sly blue eyes would turn dark when she was angry, a sure sign of a meltdown coming.

Their time was spent talking about boys and marriage proposals, and how they would go shopping in the city for dresses. Then Emily's parents had died, leaving her to care for the house, look after the small ailments of the village, and grow up much quicker than Beth.

Agony at the thought of them leaving her life bloomed from the memory and Emily felt tears run down her face. But Chris was right there, steady and anchoring at her back, and that knowledge helped her keep going.

Her mother had been a wise woman, teaching Emily about plants, herbs, and how they could help and heal people. She left big shoes to fill and Emily faltered a few times, unsure of herself. Believing she would never be as good as her mother, she read every book on healing she found and got better over time. Despite her grief and self-doubt, her knowledge grew and so did her ability. Soon, people from three villages over sought her out.

There was no one to share her successes or troubles with and she often sat at the lake, talking to it even back then. Beth had different worries, she never understood.

One day, Emily treated a boy who had stumbled into a bed of poison ivy. His rash was done with in no time, but she discovered that the child was seriously ill, past anything she could do. She pleaded with the parents to go to the city and get him help. They refused, instead offering her more money to treat him. She declined, telling them over and over that his ailment was beyond her skills. The boy died a few weeks later and the parents, lamenting his death, accused Emily of putting a curse on him.

The mayor intervened on her behalf, because she was Beth's best friend and the people soon spoke of other things. But the idea stuck. The idea that Emily's treatments were unnatural.

Everything that went wrong would be her fault. Crops failing, bad weather, animals dying... It was the witch.

When Beth's betrothed, Lukas, called on her with a supposed wound, he made advances toward her. The man told her how she wouldn't find anyone else and if she slept with him from time to time, he would make sure she was fed throughout the winter. Outraged, she threw him out. Sobbing and railing she told Beth about what happened, but instead of believing her, her friend turned on her, asking why she would be so cruel and bewitch her betrothed.

Beth's accusation and Lukas backing her story spread like wildfire and sealed Emily's fate.

The whole village came for her that night, tearing her from her home and carrying her to the stake.

All faces she knew, all of them demanding her death. All of them vile and scared. Then there was fire.

Emily screamed, clawing at the strong arms holding her. "You're okay, Em. I still got you."

Feeling him close, she endured the memory, faced the pain, the betrayal and the terror.

Heat. Scorching flames, eating. Hungry. Hissing and popping. Then darkness descended upon her. But it didn't last. The first thing she felt was cold. Soothing, cool water. Deep. Steady. Powerful. A thrum rattling her awake. Floating weightless she had come to, then searing agony coated her entire being. Her bones mended, her muscles and skin grew back, her lungs expanded and breathed water. Hacking and wheezing, she had moved, swam to shore and expelled the water in her throat.

Her skin was smooth, unmarred by fire. Emily lay on the bank, her feet still in the water, as the power from the deep swept her up. Wave after wave of sheer wrath consumed her. Dark, dangerous.

They had killed the only one worthy. Ravished the forest to make their little stick-houses. They spilled their waste into the deep, burned down trees to grow bland crops. They held animals to do their bidding, dulling their energies until nothing but mush was left inside them. Righteous and empowered to the very brim and past, she stood from the bank and headed for the houses.

Emily had forgotten. Oh, blissful ignorance… As she remembered the one thing, she had buried deeper than anything else, she was thunderstruck. The lake had driven her, taking over her body to exact revenge. Imbued with limitless rage and strength, she had swept through the village like a hurricane. Killing everyone in her sight, leveling houses and disposing of everyone. She became the one thing they had all accused her of – a blight to be feared.

Carnage and chaos. Death and utter obliteration. The rage, the insurmountable rage.

Emily shook as the images pelted her like hailstones. She cried as she rode along witnessing what she had done – what the lake had made her do. There was no telling how much of the rage burning through her was her own, but she knew one thing – she had not been in control. And she had not wanted the control back.

****

Emily slumped in his arms, her hands dropping from where they had clawed into him, leaving dents in the half-moon shape of her nails. And still her tears flowed. Silently. He reached out a bit to gauge how she was doing and pulled back with a hiss. Devastation. Deep and complete. She seemed broken.

He gathered his confidence and looked again. His heart broke for her when her usual steady pulse of energy was nothing but a splintered mess. "What have I done?" he whispered. "Em? Can you hear me, sweetheart?"

No answer.

"Shit. Em, come on, open your eyes." He shook her.

A sniffle was all the reaction he got.

"What is going on? What happened?" Chris bent to the side and pulled her onto his lap, letting her head sink against his chest. With one hand, he lifted her chin to look at her face. It was blank. Her eyes, though open, stared into nothingness.

"Emily?" He stroked her cheeks and searched her blank face for any kind of reaction. "Come back, Em."

Her lips parted and stricken sounds gushed forth. Those ever-swirling eyes of hers looked dull and empty, but they eventually focused on him. "I... I killed them. All of them."

"Who are you talking about, sweetheart?"

"The ones who burned me. I was healed and overcome by the lake. We killed them." The swirling of her irises flickered like a lightbulb. "No. There were some..." She frowned, seemingly struggling with a

146

memory. "Some I just drove out. Took back control before we reached them." A shudder crept over her and her lids slid shut. "I took back control. The innocent lived." With a shaky breath, she collapsed into him and no words or shaking woke her.

After countless minutes – the sun had sunken past the trees already – Chris picked her up and carried her home.

He was very careful to not slip and fall as he ascended the steep hill and laid her down on her pallet. Her eyes moved behind her lids rapidly. All he could do for her now was keep watch and let her rest.

****

Emily woke to his smell surrounding her. He was right behind her, hugging her to him. She nestled deeper into the embrace and rubbed her cheek against his hand. Her chest was heavy, her eyes stung, and her limbs felt leaden. The echo of her memories sang through her very bones, etching their truth into her. They had killed so many. But she had eventually fought back, wrestling control from the lake to spare the innocent. It was a small consolation in all she had experienced though.

While she watched the sky grow pale, she wept quietly, feeling like she was openly bleeding out. No wonder she had not remembered. No wonder her mind had shielded her from what she had done.

Her lake… the lake she loved so deeply. The one constant she had protected and shared her life with. Her salvation and her doom.

Chris' face slid into her hair and he sighed deeply, his breaths even and deep. Fast asleep. More tears flowed. For him. He was trapped here now, too. Had died and hit the waters, same as her, just to be resurrected to a life he probably did not want.

As sadness and anger on his behalf ran amok in Emily's veins, she was faced with a question – Why protect the lake? Why even care? It had given her power and life, but had used her to slaughter those she had known since childhood.

She groaned and stuck her nose into Chris' palm. She would very much like to hide here forever, in this cave and his arms. Both of which felt like home by now.

Chapter Seventeen

Something moved against him. Emily. He knew by her unmistakable scent of grass and honeysuckle. With sluggish ease, he reached for her energy-pulse – something he had done frequently during the night – and found that its beat was still ragged and weak, but not as bad as before.

He almost jumped from his skin when he felt her energy brush his softly, as if asking for a connection. She was awake.

Heart hammering like crazy, he allowed their pulses to mingle into one another. What he found was indescribable. A vastness of hurt, sadness and guilt raked through the connection.

Thank you, her voice thrummed in his mind.

"I am sorry," he said, hugging her close. "I shouldn't have–"

"*You held me together and allowed me to feel safe while reliving. You have nothing to apologize for.*" She laced her fingers with his and placed their fists close to her heart. "Do you want to see?" she asked, her voice gravelly.

"Only if you feel like showing me."

"I might never have the courage to ask again, but yes, I want you to know exactly who you are stuck with."

"That sounds ominous."

"It is. And so much more."

I'm ready, he thought at her, not sure if she could hear him.

She nodded once and pressed his fist closer. Then he was sucked into her energy stream completely. He saw through her eyes, feeling her life. Knowing it as she led him through it. His anger grew at how she was treated and when they came for her, he felt like yelling at the top of his lungs, like fighting every single one of those douchebags to save her. She only let him see a glimpse of the fire, but his rage doubled hearing her screams for mercy. It cut to a cold feeling of floating and waking in the lake.

Anger was next. Unfathomable, searing anger. He felt her getting overtaken by it, recognizing the pulse of the lake, the iron control it wrapped her up in, to do its bidding.

Chris was stunned as he followed her fight, the sheer force she unleashed on those who wronged her, the way she fought the lake when it turned her on the ones who couldn't fight back. She broke free, banishing them forever instead.

Sucking in a breath, he was expelled from her memories, coming back to the cave, Emily in his arms, who was dead silent, waiting for something.

"Em? Are you…"

"No. I am far from fine, or okay, as you would put it. Very, very far." She twisted in his hold and propped herself up on one elbow to look at him. Her swirling eyes teary, she stroked her fingers over his cheek. "I am so very sorry this happened to you, too. I know you want to leave. You never asked for any of this, but I wanted you to know me. What I have done. I need you to understand." A single tear ran down her face and he caught it with a finger. "And if you want me to get out of your way from now on, I will. The forest is big enough to avoid one another."

Chris raised his brows at her. "No, don't even think like that. I am neither afraid of you, nor appalled by what you did." He drew closer. "I would have killed all

150

of them myself for what they did to you. And I do understand. Deeply. I know exactly who you are. And I wouldn't want to be stuck with anyone else for eternity."

He palmed her face and tugged her down, to rest his forehead against hers. "Sleep now, I can feel how tired you are. I'll keep watch."

Emily slid down, scooting closer to him, using his bicep as a cushion. A sigh floated from her. "Thank you. For everything." Her voice got drowsy and within moments, she was fast asleep. Through their touching energies, Chris noticed how exhausted she truly was, a bone-deep tiredness took hold of her, claiming her. He pulled back to keep it from infecting him.

Holding her tightly in his arms, he let her sleep, his mind running. He could barely fathom what she'd shown him. How was one person supposed to deal with all of… that? It truly was no wonder she had drowned out those memories. His own life seemed meek and even happy in comparison.

He pecked the top of her head and an overwhelming sense of wanting to protect her arose. No matter how long it took, he would learn and grow, becoming strong enough to face anyone wanting to do her harm. As the day turned from golden to blinding outside, something clicked into place inside him. A strange feeling swirled through him and it took Chris a while to identify it. Because he didn't know the feeling. It was safety, paired with trust and understanding. And a strangely off-putting joy.

He traced a strand of her coppery hair where it curled over her upper arm. Was this what falling in love was like? Was that what he was feeling? If so, it was an unbefitting way to describe it, so much so that he couldn't be sure. All he knew was that he cared for her. And heaven help anyone meaning her harm.

****

Emily stretched her limbs, her hands searching for the comfort of a warm, soft yet firm body. They were met with blankets instead. When she blinked her eyes open all she had lived through came crashing into her at once and she sat up. The weight of her memories threatened to crush her, but she breathed through them, nearly choking on a few. It took a long time for her to find a grasp on reality through the tumult boiling and singeing her mind. To register that the sun had set and stars twinkled from the black sky, greeting her from beyond the cave entrance. But somehow, she did.

With both hands, she rubbed over her lids furiously, as if that was going to help erase what she had sought out. As if anything would ever make it go away again. Why even confront it?

Her fists sank into her lap and she glanced around. "Chris?" Only the echo of her own, thin voice floated back to her from the cave walls. She patted the blanket next to her, feeling its subtle, lingering warmth. He could not be far. With sluggish movements, she unfurled the blanket from her body and got up. When she reached the entrance, she let one hand glide up the porous limestone wall, her fingers skimmed over small cracks in the stone, following the way they spiderwebbed in every direction.

There it was, glittering innocently in the starlight. The lake. Magnificent. Its surface clear as a mirror. No mist coated it, just perfect stillness. Dread grabbed her throat, making her hands fly to pat her skin, searching for something physical, hindering her from breathing. Her fingers clasped at emptiness. Hot tears rolled down her face. Her lake. Her companion through all these years.

152

Her confidant. The source of her power, of her very life… It had used her.

Still struggling to breathe, she scrambled down the hill, her body unusually clumsy and heavy. She did not spread out her energy or listen to any of the thousand beats bouncing at the soles of her feet. Her objective became clearer the further she went down, sharpened by outrage and blind sadness. There were answers she needed.

Emily reached the forest and followed one of the countless paths she had walked along unnumbered times. To her lonely ledge, where she could only hear the falling water. The very tip of her lake, where the small falls birthed it.

Her feet felt leaden on the soft grass and she slowed the closer she got, knowing it was impossible to receive what she needed so badly. And yet, she trudged on, climbing up the ledge and walking to its very end. Gracelessly, she flopped down, letting her heavy feet dangle close to the water. Reproachfully, she glared at the lake spreading out before her in all its shiny beauty. Everything about it made her want to react as usual. With love. Even its cool smell nudged at her heart, wanting to provide comfort and joy. But she would not be wooed.

"You have some explaining to do," she said. "Why?"

As always, she was greeted with silence. And anger surged in her gut. "Fine. I will make you answer. I am done being complacent. You will hear my plight, and you will give me a reason." Gathering all her resolve, she stretched out one foot and submerged it in the lake, while reaching for the thrum of the lake itself. Emily rarely connected to the lake, safe for the special night and when she had to use the power to heal an animal or attack. Its force was too vast, too monumental to understand. Even those brushes against it to share the power hardly made sense. Doing it solely for the purpose to connect was like looking directly at the sun. Too much.

But she simply needed to know. Slipping her dress over her head, she slid from the ledge and was welcomed by the cool, dark water. Diving under, she sank, blowing air up to keep from resurfacing. With all her might, her sadness, her pain, and her disappointment, she launched her being against the essence of the lake. Shiny silver, luminescent blue, glimmering green. The colors exploded around her, bleeding from and into her.

Opening her arms and her entire self to it, she fused with the lake. *Why?* The question echoed through the bottomless deep. As the sheer, blinding consciousness of the lake suffused her, she felt her muscles tighten, ready to snap at a moment's notice. Radiating power drummed at her from all sides. Her skin, her mind, her insides. Until she was sure her bones vibrated with the hum.

Every part of her wanted to shrink back, disconnect, stop, but she held herself open. *Why?* The colors around her shone and swirled, while the languid and ancient consciousness weighed her. There was pain, the likes of which she could barely understand, even after knowing what she did. The feeling clashed against her like a thunderstorm, ripping screams of agony from her in bubbles of shiny oxygen. Then it slipped back, next was sadness. Bottomless, hopeless, hurting. Despair so unending it made her soul drown. The kind no one could live with. Even the thought of carrying it for any amount of time made her want to die.

Why? she screamed, unwilling to back down, no matter the cost. The pressure on her lungs grew, demanding air.

Loneliness. Pulling at the fabric of her sanity. A clawing, gaping emptiness, unable to be filled.

The consciousness reeled them in, shielding Emily from the feelings.

Why? she sobbed, helplessly surrendering to the pressure to breathe. But no water entered her lungs, and the pressure elevated, taking away the need to breathe altogether.

Flickers of the feelings engulfing her before ran over her, in the same order. The loneliness lingered, leading to her tears mixing with the water.

A sound reached her. Singing, laughing, brabbling words without meaning. Emily recoiled when she recognized her own voice. The sounds were coupled with warmth, relieving the pain, the sadness and the loneliness. What felt like cool fingers skimmed over her skin, then through it, as though she herself was made from water. Soft strokes. Gentle. Loving.

Warmth and joy lit up in and around her, permeating everything with such elation, she felt like floating on a blanket of those very feelings made corporeal.

The cold finger poked her chest, dipping into it and stroking over her heart. Emily stared into the colors, awestruck as she understood. I filled you with those? She asked. I relieved the darkness?

Warmth swirled through her, affirming.

The vast consciousness billowed with anger, reddening until Emily floated through what looked like blood. Rage as hot and unforgiving as the fire she had been exposed to roared around her. Her own screams sounded in her ears, her unanswered pleads for mercy. The rage twisted into dark wrath, infinite in its cruelness.

They took me from you, and the darkness threatened to come back. Warmth splintered apart the dark fury. *So, you sought vengeance, for the both of us.* More swirling warmth, turning the black back to blue, green and sliver. Cold fingers ran up Emily's energy, numbing it with its touch, soothing and covering up everything she felt.

You took my memories. To protect me.

Affirming warmth.

Floating in the vastness of her lake, she was embraced by something deeply moving. A teary feeling. So desperate and strong, it thrummed with dull yet beautiful pain. Absolute love. Unconditional and never ending. Bathed by love and gratitude, Emily was lifted and finally her head broke through the veil of the water. She opened her mouth and air raced into her lungs, stinging painfully. The connection lingered a moment longer, tugging at her with playful lovingness, before drifting away and out of her reach. The colors shimmering and glinting through the night dimmed and faded.

Stunned beyond words, Emily let her feet drift up and lay back, floating through the dark and cool waters, joining the thousands of twinkling mirror images of stars.

Somewhere an owl hooted, then the quiet whoosh of a stealthy wingbeat sailed over Emily.

Chapter Eighteen

Chris sat on the bank of the lake, staring at the display the lake and Emily had showcased. He had been patrolling the edge of the forest, feeling for any intruders, when an epic thrum reached him. As he ran toward whatever was causing, he was joined by animals, also drawn to the same place. The lake.

Surrounded by rabbits, the doe and her fawn, a family of foxes and a massive wild boar, he witnessed pure magic.

Even at this distance, he saw the swirling colors encapsulating Emily, changing as overwhelming feelings beat against him. They correlated, telling a story, along with Emily's voice. She had connected directly to the lake and it had answered in the most mind-blowing way.

Absent-mindedly he stroked the rabbit sitting next to him, his eyes wide and unblinking. How was this real? How was she real?

When she breached the surface, the colors dimmed and she floated in the dark, he let out a long breath. His heart positively hammered in his ribcage, his mind struggling to rationalize what he had experienced. But there was no rationalizing, no sense. The only thing he could do was accept it.

One by one, the animals left, small and big feet crunching on the pebbles as they turned back to the shelter of their forest. The rabbit nudged his palm once with a wriggling nose, then hopped away, too.

Chris stayed and waited, watching Emily hover in the twinkling blackness. There was no telling how long she floated and he grew anxious and worried, more than once he got close to swimming to her, but something held him back. This was her moment.

He passed the time with building little, wobbly towers out of pebbles. His thoughts seemed shocked into silence, happy with the simple task of watching Emily and building pebble towers.

Little splashes sounded and she finally swam to shore. Chris had no trouble feeling Emily's energy. The steady pulse he had come to know her by was back. Stronger than before.

A smile grew on his lips when she walked from the water. And while he was – as always – hit by how she looked, he didn't avert his eyes. Instead, they were glued to her body. Droplets twinkled on her long, toned legs as she strode over with impossible grace. Her whole body moved too smooth to be human. The subtle muscles of her belly clenched and released, her perfect breast swayed subtly and her swirling eyes glowed with the same shimmering colors the lake had been illuminated by.

Dripping wet, she stretched out a hand to him, water droplets hitting his legs. He took it and was yanked to his feet with seemingly no effort at all.

"You saw?" she asked.

All he managed was a nod. He laced their fingers, unable to take his gaze from her. "You okay?"

"I will be," she said, her voice as melodic and enchanting as the first night he met her. And he could see it. The calm she radiated was entwined with all she had lived through, but it shone through, steadfast and unbroken.

****

Emily lived through the next day in a strange headspace. She still felt like she was floating in her lake, was sucked back into that moment frequently and often stared into the distance. The only thing taking her out of it was him. Chris coaxed words, teachings and even smiles from her.

If not for him, she would have lost herself to a constant loop of reliving. And there was no telling when, or if, she would have snapped out of it. Her limbs, though light, felt stuck in that floating sensation, and while she marveled at what and how the lake had showed its reasoning, she knew why she had never tried to connect with it directly before. The experience had almost been too much to come back from.

"Em?"

She blinked and faced him. "I apologize."

A cheeky grin lit up his handsome face. "I only had to call you twice this time. You are getting better." The lines around his eyes, a byproduct of his grin, highlighted his green irises beautifully.

Emily dug her fingers into the sand underneath the pebbles, trying to ground herself in the moment and not drift off.

Chris picked up one of the pebbles, turned it over and scrutinized it with drawn brows. He stood and bounced the pebble from his hand only to catch it again with ease. The he leaned back, twisting his shoulder and torso, before letting the pebble fly and skip over the lake.

Inadvertently, Emily's gaze settled on the hem of his pants. The moment he threw the stone, it dipped a bit, showing off a tan line that set off the sun-kissed skin of his back. A shivery tug went through her lower belly, eliciting a fluttering breath to blow from her lips. For the first time since he had helped her brave her past, she saw him the way she usually did.

He pulled one hand through his slightly too long hair. By now it curled around the nape of his neck. Begging her fingers to thread through it.

"Did you see that? Twenty bounces." He turned, making the stones at his feet scamper over one another. The tug was back, stronger than before. Emily dusted off her palms on her knees and got to her feet. She singled out a flat stone and threw it up once to catch it, like he had. "Step aside, beginner."

He smirked and raised a brow. "Okay, Miss Fancydress, show me what you got."

Emily mimicked his twist and turn. "One, two, three, four-five-six-seven-eight… twenty-five… thirty!" Joy sang in her chest, pushing at the lethargy and she skipped in a circle, celebrating her win and the elongated period of clarity.

Arms came around her and she yelped in surprise as he swung her around. Her feet lifted and she flung out a small pebble that had been stuck between her toes. With a teensy splash, it hit the water.

Emily's hands flew to his holding her and the tug was joined by a prickling sensation, spreading from her hands and up her arms.

Chris sat her down, with her head swimming a little, but he still held onto her. With a smile, she let her back sink against his chest.

"More of this, Em. Come back to me," he rumbled close to her ear, making pleasant shivers scamper up her lower back.

"I…" The thought trailed off as things shifted out of focus, like it had multiple times during the night and day.

Her body was twirled in his arms and his face registered in her view. That beautiful face.

With both palms he cupped her cheeks. "Em?" His brows drew together with worry. "Tell me how to help you."

As he drifted in and out of focus for a few heartbeats, Emily still felt the delicious prickling sensation his palms made erupt on her cheeks. His searching eyes also added to the tug, whisking her back from where she drifted off.

She wanted this to last, to feel him clearly, to live in this moment with him. Emily surged forward and fused her lips to his. Clarity bombarded the lethargy, driving it to the very back of her mind.

For a moment, he stilled with surprise, then his fingers sank into her hair and he groaned against her lips, moving them on hers. *Sliding, soft, firm.* Emily closed her eyes and gave herself over to the heat roaring to life inside her.

With resounding suddenness, she was hit with detail. The late sun caressing her shoulders, the sound of rippling water behind her, chirping birds, a dove cooing, wind combing through leaves. Her hair, slipping off her shoulder, tickling as it went. And him.

Her lids slid shut and she surrendered to the pull leading to him. Emily skimmed her hands up his naked back, not able to get enough of his soft firmness.

Their kiss deepened, sending tremors over her being, the way his lips moved on hers was maddening. She pressed her entire body to his, needing more, wanting him closer. Her nails dug into his shoulders and she moaned when he trembled against her. A firm hardness rested on her belly, making need pool at her core. Almost painful.

He pulled away, gasping for air. His green eyes searched her face. "Emily," he rasped. "This is madness."

"The good kind," she whispered, rising to her tiptoes to continue her exploration. When he pulled back, she dropped down. "I want to feel you, all of you. You keep it all at bay."

"Jeez, Em. You must know by now what you do to me. But this insane need I have for you..." He swallowed, his breath heavy. "I don't know if I can stop once–"

"I understand what I want. I know that neither of us will be able to stop." She took his hand and placed his palm to her chest. "Know that I want you. I feel the same way you do." Similar words in a similar situation, which felt long ago but was not. Only their roles had been reversed.

She licked her lips, her ragged breath burning in her throat. "Kiss me. Take me. Make me feel real again."

With something close to a growl, he sank his lips to hers. Gone was the soft sliding and held-back passion. His energy brushed up to hers, twining, mingling, sending her need soaring.

His hands were everywhere, squeezing, stroking, clasping her to him, and she clawed at him with the same burning need. The same desperation.

Their lips moved as though dancing, then he nipped at her lower lip, sucked it into his mouth and drew his tongue over it. She moaned and her legs nearly gave out when what felt like sparks of lightning forked over her skin.

He let go and coaxed her mouth open with his tongue. His taste was an explosion. Velvety smoothness. Sliding heat. Her head swam as she drank him in, deciding then and there that she would never get enough of his taste. Tingle after tingle vibrated through her as they stumbled further up the bank, unable to let go of one another or stop kissing.

Strong fingers hooked the dress from her shoulders and it whispered down her body. She stepped from it and hissed when her skin met his. Her hunger for him turned carnal and she gasped as his hands slid down her back and dug into her butt, pulling her lower body firmly against his hardness.

Their breaths mingled, short and raw. Every stroke of skin left a tingle that added to the pooling heat, every taste of him blasted her higher. His smell of sun-kissed skin and cool water crazed her. The feel of his muscles, his skin, his hair, singed her palms with heat. His heart hammered right above hers, pressed so close to him she felt it beat as rapidly as hers.

His hands on her butt tightened and he picked her up, turned and bent down to place her on the soft grass. Dimly, Emily recognized it as the same hill she had dragged him to after pulling him from the lake on the night they met.

Cool grass hit her naked back as he hovered over her, pulling back a little to look at her. His green eyes had darkened with lust and Emily reached up to cup his face. She let her fingers roam over his skin, the curves of his mouth, his stubbly jaw – not scratchy anymore but soft – his straight nose, his brows. Sliding her hand into the sheer softness of his curls, she pulled him down, conquering his lips, marking them as hers.

His palms skimmed her side, making her breath hitch. His lips left hers to kiss a path down her jaw, to her neck, sending bouts of shivers over her entire body. As if she had turned into a blank nerve, she felt everything with staggering intensity. His breath on her skin was warm, causing her pulse to race. With his hands and mouth, he explored her while she threaded her fingers through his hair, arching up to his touch and moaning softly.

Hot lips grazed her breasts, sending shocks of want down her stomach. And deeper. Emily felt his struggle to be gentle in the way his hands shook slightly.

"You're beautiful, Em," he rasped between licks and kisses, his energy spiking with lust.

She wanted more, needed more. But he took his time, tormenting her with his fiery, languid touch. Her body came to life beneath his caresses, until she was a knot of trembling need.

"More," she managed to groan.

A chuckle, tickling the skin under her left breast answered and his hands stroked a little firmer, his teeth nibbled and tugged, stinging deliciously.

With an aggravatingly low pace, he worked his way down her body. The small bites on her hipbones, soothed with impossibly soft kisses, made her squirm with anticipation.

One of his large hands slid up and down her thighs, then gently opened them.

Emily gasped and lifted her head to see what he was doing. Their eyes met as he positioned himself between her legs, his shoulders brushing her thighs. He smiled, looking devilishly handsome, before lowering his face.

Her head fell back as goosebumps raked her skin. Fingers parted her, making way for his lips, his tongue… Emily's hands hit the grass next to her, they clenched and unclenched as he drew his tongue up and down her center. Wet heat, sliding perfection, tingling ecstasy.

She gasped for air when everything she felt concentrated on that single touch between them both, pulsing with sensation, transcending anything she would have ever imagined.

His swirling tongue was joined by stroking fingers, gingerly dipping into her. The feeling was foreign. Exquisite.

Her legs shook around his head with involuntary tremors as she lay there, unable and unwilling to stop the waves of sensations crashing through her. Muscles tightened, breath stopped, allowing for absolute focus. Tense from head to toe she received him. Building, climbing, until… His name tumbled from her lips in a cry when her body released all of its tension in one moment. Blasts of prickling heat rolled through her, making her body convulse.

Chris grabbed her legs to stay in place, forcing her to ride out every nuance of pleasure, every minute shiver of passion. Shivering waves crashed against her skin, carrying her through the most intense high she'd ever known.

Eventually, her body calmed and her frantic breath slowed, her heart pounded like crazy and Emily stared at the blue sky above her, not seeing a thing, shocked with the expanse of what Chris had made her feel.

He crawled up her body and she immediately pulled him closer, kissing those devilish lips of his until he was the one groaning. Emily pushed him to the side and he landed on his back with a surprised grunt. Quick as a cat, she was on top of him. Her pale hands spanned over his chest, looking tiny as she relished his soft firmness.

"My turn," she said, her voice warped with lust. Chris brows shot up, but he did not object.

Tingling with the aftereffects of blasting straight into the sky, Emily learned him. Every ridge of muscle, each piece of skin, small freckles, scars – all of him. His taste was honey on her tongue and down her throat. His smell coating her until it was all she perceived. The repressed moans she elicited with her exploration thrummed through her innards and stoked the hunger she felt for him.

Little by little, she worked her way down his body, as he had done with her. There was no hesitation when she touched, kissed and tasted him, her mind was burdened with one focus. Chris. His eyes glinted with need when she nestled at his pants. Huffing with frustration as her jittery fingers struggled with the button and some kind of metal teeth she had never seen. She was a hairbreadth away from ripping the piece of clothing from him.

He seemed to notice, because his hands brushed hers out of the way, making quick work of opening his trousers. When he made a motion to shove them down, she slapped his hands with a growl. "My turn," Emily repeated.

Chris held up his hands, then laced his fingers behind his head, laying down on them. He grinned, then bit his lower lip, almost unearthing a second growl from her. "Be my guest," he said, his voice guttural.

Emily pulled at his pants, inching them down to reveal that charming tan line and the V-shaped muscles leading lower. She bent down to nibble at those, surprised by the smoothness of his skin. Moans and gasps accompanied her endeavors, music to her ears. She tugged the pants lower, her eyes widening when they slid off and down his legs. All of him was beautiful. Her hands ran over him and she gasped along with him. Had she been surprised at the smoothness of his skin before, she was now floored. Silken softness, paired with rigid firmness.

Dipping down, she tasted him, letting her tongue dart out and swirl, dab and play.

Chris moved underneath her, his hands shooting from behind his head to reach for hers. Each lick had an effect, every kiss was met with a barley contained thrust. She smiled, knowing she could spend hours making him react to her touch, it was amazing how receptive to her touch he was. Addictive.

His fingers dug into her hair, pressing against her scalp, sending languorous bouts of delight down her back. Her lids fluttered from the feeling and she moaned around him.

A hiss later, he pulled her up. Just as she was about to complain, she saw his face. A mask of unbridled want greeted her, sending a shockwave through her body. She leaned forward, meeting his lips with hers for a heated, breathless kiss.

"I want you," Chris rasped.

"I need you," she said at the same time.

Never breaking the kiss, he lifted her up so she straddled him. Her breath hitched when her heat met his hardness. Her body rocked back and forth, sliding over him, and she gasped. The sensation so intense that her head swam and her muscles quivered.

Chris sucked in a breath, pulled her up a bit and reached around her. Emily felt blunt hardness and rocked back a tad. Where his fingers had felt amazing, this was nearly too much.

He sank into her, stretching, filling, sliding. Stinging. She leaned forward again, away from the sting.

"Slowly, sweetheart. You are in control," Chris said with a strained voice.

Shaking with need, but wary of the stinging feeling, she stilled. "What do I do now?"

He placed one hand on her hip and rocked her back and forth gently. His other hand wound around the nape of her neck, pulling her down. While his kisses maddened her, she took more of him within her with each rocking motion. Her body adapted to his length with ease and the unusual, stimulating feeling of him filling and stretching her was unbelievable.

Soon, she moved on her own, until she sank back firmly, moaning deeply as she buried him inside of her fully. His answering groan spoke of bliss.

Emily straightened and gazed down at him. He was exquisite, his body made for hers.

Slowly, she began moving, listening to what her body wanted, falling into a rhythm older than time itself.

****

She was slippery heat. Her swirling eyes, the stuff of fairytales, bottomless depths threatening to drown him. Every inch of his being was on fire and it took all he had to let her take the lead and stay still beneath her.

Her coppery hair swayed back and forth as she moved, falling and sliding over her breasts, prompting his hands to reach up and join their caress. Her lids slid shut and her head fell back as she arched into his touch. Sliding tightness, sending tingles through him. Her excruciatingly beautiful face scrunched up with concentration, her cheeks flushed with color, her lips opened, her breath harsh. Little bites of pain raked his chest, where her nails dug into his flesh and he moaned. Emily rocked back and forth faster, undulating her hips in mind-numbing circles. There was no doubt in her eyes, nor in the pulses of her energy. It spoke of single-minded need as it mingled and danced with his own. As singular as the experience was, he forced his eyes to stay open and take in every move she made, the scope of which threatened to overwhelm him.

Chris reveled in each moan, every tiny shiver, and the feel of her engulfing him. He wanted all of it and more. And while he was dangerously close to the edge, he knew with absolute clarity that his need for her would not subside. It seemed endless as the blue sky above them.

Her hips curled faster, until she slid onto him with raw harshness, taking his breath away. Fingers clenching his skin, her face a mask of concentration, her glorious body took from him what she needed. Then she opened her eyes and yelled, tightening around him in waves.

She fell forward and he caught her, thrusting up at the same punishing pace she had put him through. Her teeth found the crook of his neck, muffling her cries as she clenched him in waves of pleasure, trembling in his arms like a leaf.

It took only a few times of surging into her, then his orgasm hit with a vengeance and he nearly saw stars. A sharp yell broke from his chest as he clutched her to him.

Her heart hammered against his chest, her breath cooled the bite on his neck and she slumped on him, going lax. Their mingling energies told of her bliss, stroking his lovingly and floating through it like silken sheets. He hugged her and breathed in her scent deeply. He was awash with her. Tasting, smelling and feeling nothing but her, he lay there, his mind quiet and serene for the first time in his life.

"I want to stay like this forever," Emily mumbled.

"Deal," Chris said.

She chuckled and snuggled closer. "Thank you."

"You're thanking me? I am the one who should be thanking you."

Gingerly, she stroked his shoulder. "When I said I needed you, I was not kidding. You woke me, brought me back. Thank you for that."

Gratitude flooded him. "Anytime."

Emily pushed herself up so she could see his face. "Promise?"

With his index finger, Chris tucked a strand of hair behind her ear. "Promise."

A radiant smile grew on her lips and she lowered he face, brushing her lips to his. Soft, giving, and unbearably gentle.

"You up for a swim?" she asked against him.

"Always." He lifted her up, plonked her down and shot up. "Race you!" he yelled when he sprinted off, laughing at her derailed expression.

Faster than humanly possible, she sprang up and gave chase, but they were the same and his speed doubled as his heart bounced in his chest with a stupidly warm joy.

His feet hit the water first, but his jeer of victory was cut off when she tackled him, sending them both into the cool water.

They came up laughing and spluttering, hovering weightlessly. Her arms circled him, those swirling eyes set on his lips. A tingle of heat thrummed through him and she fanned it by slinging both legs around him, effectively climbing him.

One kiss, another. Wet skin sliding against his.

"I feel like I cannot refrain from touching you," she said, then kissed him again. "Nor from kissing you. It makes my heart bounce and my skin tingle." Resting her elbows on his shoulders, she pressed her entire body to his. "This fornication thing is amazing. How does one stop?"

Chris laughed and grabbed her ass. He shimmied her down to let her feel just what her antics had woken. "Who said one has to?"

171

Chapter Nineteen

Wide awake she lay under the stars. Her body buzzed with satisfaction, feeling thoroughly loved. Emily finally understood the term 'making love.' It was appropriate. She let her head drop to the side, gazing at Chris. He was fast asleep, lying next to her on their little hill of grass. Her heart swelled with a strange ache and the corners of her lips lifted. Yes, she loved this man, this annoying, caring, wonderful man. He had met her disdain with kindness, her strangeness with understanding, and her demons with embraces and soothing closeness. The only thing worrying her was that he was imprisoned here. If only she could pay him back by freeing him. As hard as it would be on her, she would give anything for him to be happy and untethered. But there was naught she could do. Shaking off her musings, she sighed and rolled her head back to look at the sky. The full moon was a week away, but she could not wait to show it to Chris. To swim with him in illuminated blue, glowing green and shiny silver.

Sitting up, she smirked at a firefly as it blinked by. The familiar sound of small ripples on pebbles mixed with the one of Chris' breaths. Pulling her knees up, she hugged them to her and rested her chin on them. Of their own volition, her toes started digging at the dirt under the grass. The similarity to the night she had met him was not lost to her, but she could not have felt more different. Could not be more different. Chris had rattled her world, and while it would take time to overcome what he had unearthed, she would never choose to go back.

The night around her was clear, free from the lethargy the lake had left her with and Emily filled her lungs to bursting with a deep breath, enjoying what she felt. She spread her hands on the grass and opened herself up to feel.

Thousands of pulses reached her, those close and those far away. Small ones, large ones, and quick ones. Knowing them all, Emily swayed from side to side, following their melody.

Something strange brushed her, a sharp prickle she could not identify. She frowned and concentrated. Brittle and spiky, coming from the direction of the old oak. It did not feel threatening or bad, but she needed to investigate. For beings to enter, whom she did not know, was rare.

With a quick glance at Chris, she decided to let him sleep, she had worn him out enough today. Swiftly, she rose and strode across the hill and into the forest. The foreign pulse had not moved, but it felt wrong, afraid? Falling into a jog, trusting her feet to find her way, she crossed through the forest. It still took a while and the closer she got, the more chitter-chatter filled the air and the louder the other pulses got. Eventually, she heard a rattling growl coming from the direction of the oak. Not menacing, more scared than anything else. Emily hurried on, needing to know what made that noise.

Countless nightbirds sat in the trees, hooting and screeching, seemingly as confused as she was.

Then she reached the oak and halted immediately. Something metallic stood at the roots of the tree. Emily knew that if she got too close, the searing pain would consume her, so she tentatively snuck closer.

The rattling growl grew louder, followed by a clatter. It… it came from the metallic thing. She squinted and saw that it was a cage, housing a small animal who threw its body against the metal bars, making it clatter.

Sensing its plight and fear, Emily sidled closer, feeling for any other energies. But no one was around. The cage was human made, and a human had to have put it there, but none were around.

"Who put you in there?" she asked, getting down on all fours to see better and be less frightening. The cage rattled as the animal jumped at the bars to get away from her.

"No, no, dear. Calm down. You will hurt yourself." Slowly, the burning sensation crept over her skin as she crawled on, but she bit her teeth together and went on. She had to free the frightened little one. Emily pushed her energy outward in a calming ripple and the rattling growl calmed, the cage stilled.

A fluffy coat of black and gray fur appeared. Beady eyes, decorated by a black mask, twinkled from the cage. Tiny black paws gripped the bars caging it in. One last growl showed off a row of sharp, white teeth.

"There you go. I will help you." Step by step, she moved further. All the while the pain ratcheted up. Sweat broke from her forehead and ran down her cheeks as she hissed and forced her body on. The pain turned to agony, then to scalding torment. Her breaths were shallow as she finally reached the cage. With a hand she grabbed hold and pulled it. Something snapped and a net shot from the ground, flinging her into the air, the cage in her arms. The agony lessened as the net was hung a bit further from the border than the cage had been placed.

A trap. Emily swung from side to side in the net, telling her shock and closely following anger to simmer down. She had been in those before. And as her perusal had told her, there were no humans around. She had time. Calmly, she fiddled open the cage. The masked animal climbed out and scampered up the net. It chittered a bit while it pushed through a hole in the net and climbed further up the rope to vanish between leaves and branches.

"You are welcome, tiny captive," Emily yelled. She dug her fingers between the ropes of the net and tore it apart with ease. Seconds later, she slid from it, catching her fall with a roll. The moment her soles fused with the forest ground, a sharp jab surged through her. A warning from the lake. It felt frighteningly weak.

"Christian," she gasped, and ran, following the jabbing urgency.

****

"Don't move, asshole," a cold voice said. Chris jerked awake and found himself at the receiving end of a gun barrel. Gus' angry face bore down at him from behind the gun he was pointing.

With a quick glance, Chris assessed two things – Emily was gone, and he was surrounded by eight of Gus' men.

"Didn't we kill him?" the meek voice of Clarence asked.

"Shut it, shithead," Gus snapped.

"My question is, why is he naked?" another one asked.

"Cause he got it on with the red-head."

Laughter ensued.

Scalding wrath coated Chris with lightning speed. They had watched Emily and him somehow.

"I said, shut it," Gus roared. His eyes glittered with disdain and he snapped the fingers of his free hand. "Did we get her?" he asked.

Clarence tapped the screen of his smartphone, his gaunt face illuminated by the ghostly glow of the screen. "Uhm… She ripped open the net and is on her way here… Arndt wants to know if he should take the shot."

Leaden fear slid into Chris' gut. "No," he whispered.

Gus scowled. "Yeah. Tell him to dart her."

Spreading his fingers over the grass, Chris sent out waves of warnings, hoping to high heaven that Emily understood.

"What do we do with him?" one of the goons asked, jerking his chin at Chris.

"What we should have done in the first place," Gus drawled, cocking the gun. "Only this time, I'll blast away his pretty face." A cruel grin sliced into his face. "Thanks to fate, I get to kill you all over again. How quaint."

Chris reached for the power of the lake. Emily hadn't shown him exactly how to work it, but he would make due with what he knew. There was a jab, flashing far into the forest, but it was weak, sluggish. It felt tired. Chris remembered Emily telling him that the force was finite, replenished during the full moon. Had the lake's interaction with Emily drained it? It seemed impossible. He had felt the vastness during helping the doe. How could something so overwhelmingly powerful be drained?

"Gus," Clarence said, his voice thin.

"What? I am about to enjoy a moment over here."

"Yeah, you might want to hold that thought. Arndt says she left his reach."

"Impossible. Did he hit her?"

"Y-yes. But she just kept going."

Chris smiled as his pulse vibrated against hers. Dark rage, unstoppable. "You shouldn't have come," he said.

"Shut up, bitch," Gus said, his finger wrapping around the trigger.

"Jesus! Boss, you might wanna–"

Everyone turned toward the forest. She walked from the trees, the little light provided by the growing moon was sucked away around her, making it appear as if she walked from a black hole. Wind whisked up leaves around her, letting her hair dance from her pale shoulders.

"You will leave now," her voice echoed with dark rage and power.

"Stay where you are, girly," Gus said. "Or this guy is toast. For real this time."

Emily's swirling eyes flew to him, her pulse skimming over his, worry prominent. And a dull numbness, growing steadily. *Are you... okay?* her voice sounded in his mind.

I am. Run, Em. They will kill you if you don't.

Her face tightened and her gaze rose to Gus. *Not a chance.* "You think coming here was a good idea?" she asked. "You think threatening him will keep you alive?" Pulling small darts from her upper shoulder and neck. *Clink, clink, clink.* Their sound on the pebbles floated over the short distance as she strutted closer. "You think this," Emily held up the last dart, "will keep me from tearing you limb from limb?" *Clink.*

"Fucking hell," one of the men whispered. "That much should have sent an Elephant to la-la-land."

"Stop, woman!" Gus yelled, his hand trembling slightly as the gun barrel swiveled slightly.

With each step Chris felt Emily weaken further, the darts worked, consuming her energy with that dull numbness he had felt from her before.

"You will leave now. This is your last chance." She stumbled and the wind mellowed down. Even the darkness surrounding her lessened with a flicker.

"No. This was yours, girly." Gus pulled the trigger and Chris leaned to the side with inhuman speed, feeling the bullet scrape his cheek and whistle past his ear. The shot rang over the lake, silencing the night. Believing to have hit his mark, Gus raised his gun to line it up with Emily, who stumbled on but fell to her knees.

In the space of a heartbeat, Chris remembered her dying screams, the people who had damned her to death, the ones who had tried to hurt her since. And the ones who would still try to, like these assholes. Unholy wrath sang in his veins, connecting him firmly with the slow, deep pulse of the lake. Red coated his vision as he let out a roar, rising to his feet.

Gus jerked around, his gun going off too low. The bullet entered Chris' stomach, little more than a sting. Balling his fist, he sent it flying, catching Gus under his chin. The man's neck was thrown back by the force and snapped with an ugly crack.

All hell broke loose as guns went off, men screamed and wrath drenched Chris' world further. He felt tiny stings on his body, but he was quick and his hands grabbed, punched and tossed the men surrounding him as if they were mere puppets. His fists slick with blood, he raged through the group, chasing those down who ran for their lives. No one had a chance.

His feet told him where each one was, and when he let the last one – Clarence – slump from his grasp, more footsteps rippled from the forest. The ones who had shot Emily. He let out another roar and ran for them. They did not see him coming as he plowed into them. The one who carried a long rifle tried to run, but he was first. Chris grabbed him by the throat and smashed his face into a tree. Dodging a wild swing to his face from another with ease, he rammed his shoulder into the man's unprotected belly, making his ribs crack. Whirling around, he kicked the last one with such force that he took off and hit a broad pine tree with his back. Feeling their energies flicker and die, Chris huffed and hurried back to the bank.

Mangled bodies lay strew around Emily, who had fallen to the side, succumbing to whatever kind of drug had been in those darts. Chris sank down and lifted her chin to face him, her bleary eyes threatening to add to his rage. He felt like killing them all over again.

"Em." Sliding his arms under her body, he picked her up.

"Lake," she managed to whisper.

With a nod, Chris stemmed the wrath he had tapped into and carried her to their lake. The water lapped at his feet, stroked over his legs and up his body. When it reached his hips, he sank down, and drifted on, with her still in his arms.

Listening to and stroking her pulse, he let them float deeper. The rage spilled from him in streams and the water darkened as the blood from his wounds joined it. The stings burned now. And the clearer his head got, the more they hurt.

Emily poked him weakly. "You have to take out the metal. So, the lake can heal you."

"You first. What do I do?"

That disgruntled expression he knew so well was back, but he shook his head.

"No, Em. Don't even try it. You first."

"Pull at my blood, thread out what does not belong." She pointed at the little specks of blood on her neck where the darts had hit her. "Use your hand."

With his wounds aching and throbbing he cupped his palm to her neck.

“Feel my pulse, thread out what is wrong and pull.”

Chris searched for the flow of her energy and felt gooey strings suffusing it. Moving his hand away from her neck he pulled at the strings. Nothing happened, and as he felt his strength waning, his heartrate picked up. There. Clear liquid pearled from her tiny wounds and rolled off her skin to fall into the lake.

With each drop the dull numbness lifted more.

Chapter Twenty

The frustrating numbness drifted out of her, and she got increasingly angry. As soon as she could, Emily twisted from Chris' hold. "You, crazy, stubborn man," she hissed and cupped her palm to one of his many wounds, drawing out the metal embedded in his flesh, she let it drop and moved on to the next. And the next, and the next.

"I cannot believe you took such a risk, you completely powered yourself out." Her toes hit the mud and sank deeper into the mushy softness. "I thought that first shot…" She bit down on her lower lip. Those cursed little pinpricks that had weakened her. It had nearly cost her him. Tears welled from her eyes as she worked on him, rolling from her face to mix with the blood and water floating around them.

"Careless. I should have anticipated… This is all my fault."

"Em," he said softly, but she ignored him. Swiftly pulling at more bullets.

"Holy saints, how many of those did you take?"

"Emily. I am fine."

She snorted. "You are not fine. Y-you could have… And I–"

"And you would have gotten your wish from that very first night we met."

She glared at him. "You are an idiot, Christian."

A tired smirk pulled at his exhausted face. "I know."

Emily rounded him and went to work on his back, her gaze flitted to shore, touching the vile men lying there. "This should not have happened. It is my responsibility to protect, that includes you."

"I would do it again," he said. "For you, I would watch the world burn."

Her hands stilled as he turned to her. "You do not know what you are saying."

"I love you, Emily." His eyes found hers and she froze, her heart fluttering like the wings of a hummingbird. "And the thought of losing you made me snap. I have been alone for all my life. It took dying to find you. And I will never let any harm come to you, no matter what happens or how long I live." He tilted his chin at the shore. "Those guys were my responsibility. They stumbled into this place because of me. And now, they will never bother you, or anyone else, ever again."

He stroked a strand of wet hair from her shoulder. "You are not alone anymore, like it or not. Your burdens are my burdens now."

More than anything, those words rang through her. And with those simple words, a weight inside her shifted, growing lighter.

****

A headache pierced him as soon as he opened his eyes. Blinking, he shadowed his eyes from the sun and rolled around on his pallet. He found Emily sitting on the other side of the fireplace, holding sticks with mushrooms over a small fire.

Groaning, Chris rubbed his lids and sat up. "How long was I out?"

"You lost a lot of blood. One day and one night."

She had healed him in the lake, then helped him to their cave. Soon as his head had hit the pallet, it had been lights out for him.

"You okay?" he asked.

Emily pulled one stick back and poked at the mushroom. Scowling, she placed it back. "Why do you always ask me that?"

"Because I want to know the answer. It's important to me."

"Yes. I am. Are you?"

"I feel like a warthog trampled through my brain, but other than that…"

"What is a warthog?"

Chris recoiled, cursing the movement a second later as throbbing pain shot through his head. "You don't – a warthog is a wild pig. Smaller than a boar, though." It was so easy forgetting she was from another time.

Emily gathered the mushrooms, placed them on a flat stone next to a grilled fish and picked it up. She straightened and rounded the fire, not missing a beat when one of the logs popped and crumbled in an eruption of sparks. Handing him the makeshift plate, she took a seat at his side.

"This is for me?" he asked.

She nodded.

"What about you?"

"I ate this morning. And I know how much you like grilled fish. I figured you would wake soon due to your pulse strengthening, so I thought doing the same to mushrooms would be a nice idea."

"Thanks, Em." He picked up a mushroom and blew on it before putting it in his mouth. The smokey goodness had him closing his eyes. "It's amazing." Quickly, he picked up another.

"I love you too," Emily blurted out, fiddling with the hem of her dress.

The mushroom fell from his fingers and rolled across the floor and into the fire, where it sizzled into blackness.

"I wanted you to know. Maybe this makes it easier for you being stuck here?"

He sat the plate down and pulled her on his lap. "I am happy, Em. Here. With you. You are home." She smiled and leaned in for a kiss. As before, her soft lips made his breath short.

"Me too."

For the next hour, the fish and the mushrooms were forgotten, as well as the headache.

Epilogue

Night never came easy.

Emily and Chris strolled down the bank of their lake, hands entwined. The air was abuzz with insects and the last light of day painted the ripples of the lake golden. Their chatting and laughter wove in seamlessly with the sounds of the forest and lake. Frogs croaked along, doves cooed from a poplar, and a fish jumped from the depths, raining golden droplets everywhere.

"Can you feel it?" Emily asked.

"Yes. It's a strange hum, deep in my body. Like…"

"As though your bones are singing?"

"Exactly." He shook himself a bit, making her laugh. "How do you stand it?"

"I sing along." Emily raised their twined hands and twirled in a circle, her dress fanning out at her sides. She trilled a nonsensical song, her melodic voice light and perfect in the late day.

Chris laughed and caught her around the waist, then he swung her around. She squealed happily, her naked feet skimming the surface of the lake before he sat her down.

"Still the crazy lady I met. *My* crazy lady."

She stuck out her tongue at him, then they climbed their small hill of grass. Emily stopped and turned into him, hugging him to her with all her might. The things that had happened sometimes overwhelmed her and she needed his warmth to stem the memories and thoughts. Chris cupped her face and held her gaze with his.

"I know," she said and rose to her tiptoes to kiss him. The kiss led to more and she wondered dimly whether it would ever change, if she would ever not want him. But as their bones sang unison as the special night grew closer, all she cared about was being with him.

They loved each other on the hill of grass until the moon rose from the forest and a moist chill rose from the lake.

Naked, they stood and watched as the silver light touched the surface, creating a perfect mirror image. The pull overcame both and they walked down the hill and into the water, their pulses as entwined as their hands. Illuminated blue, shiny green and glowing silver spread from them in ripples. The colors floated around them, through them, out of them.

The forest quieted down, waiting, anticipating. Even a restless, masked forager halted his search for food and regarded the glowing show.

A huge sigh expanded throughout the lake, rustling the trees with its tremor, before the bout of pressure was sucked back into the lake. The glow paled, but stayed in both their eyes, an ever-swirling mix of illuminated blue, shiny green and glowing silver.

Chris and Emily floated next to each other, reveling in the tingling energy suffusing them. Their hands touched, as did their pulses. Both had found what lacked from their lives in another. She was his home. And he was her safety. They were both Lakeborn.

THE END

Acknowledgements

Thank you, dear reader, dear dreamer, for reading this weird little book. It was a journey to write, but I loved every second and hope that love can be felt in my words. Thank you, special friend, for believing in me and always telling me that I have what it takes. You make my days better and my work more colorful.
As always, thank you Butterdragons Publishing, for believing in my work way more than I do.
To Dazed Designs. I love the cover! You outdid yourself. Again.
MJ and Joshua… Bring these weirdos to life, babes!

About Victoria Larque

Victoria Larque writes Paranormal Romance and Urban Fantasy. Her love for the genre is rooted in the fact that she has rules to go by, but they can be bent and even broken if need be. She was born and raised in the wonderful country of Namibia and is now residing and working in Germany where she lives in the woods with her adorable, grumpy husband. She has learned the amazing craft of being a car-mechanic, but her passion is writing, telling stories and dreaming up impossibilities. When she gets home from work, she writes. On the weekends she writes. Her goal is to, one day, be able to do nothing but indulge in her passion.

Other BDP books by Victoria Larque

Terrifying Love - A Halloween Anthology
Beautiful Tragedy - A Halloween Anthology
Demon Rising (Embers Duology Book One)
Angel Falling (Embers Duology Book Two)
Princess of Stone (Fractured Queendom Trilogy Book One)
Golden Tattoo A Halloween Anthology